ROAD TO REVENGE

ROAD TO REVENGE

STEVEN GRAY

A Black Horse Western

ROBERT HALE · LONDON

© Steven Gray 1993
First published in Great Britain 1993

ISBN 0 7090 4998 6

Robert Hale Limited
Clerkenwell House
Clerkenwell Green
London EC1R 0HT

The right of Steven Gray to be identified as
author of this work has been asserted by him
in accordance with the Copyright, Designs and
Patents Act 1988.

Photoset in North Wales by
Derek Doyle & Associates, Mold, Clwyd.
Printed and bound in Great Britain by
WBC Print Ltd, and WBC Bookbinders Ltd,
Bridgend, Mid-Glamorgan.

ONE

Freedom!

Beyond the tall prison gates, the dusty road beckoned. But Andrew McConnell walked hesitantly through them, as if he was almost reluctant to leave the jail's security. Ten years was a very long time and facing the outside world was suddenly daunting. Then the sound of the gate clanging shut behind him, made him realize: he'd served his time, he was no longer a prisoner.

He took a deep breath, straightened his shoulders and didn't look back.

'Don't let me see you any more,' the Warden had said earlier that morning. 'You don't belong here.'

And McConnell meant to follow that advice. He was out of prison and he didn't want to do anything that might send him back. The thoughts of revenge he'd lived with for the past ten years no longer seemed important. They vanished in the new heady feeling of release.

Below him was the untidy sprawl of huts making up the small town serving the prison. At the edge was the railroad station. Like most just released convicts, that was where McConnell headed.

He felt awkward in the cheap, ill-fitting suit provided by the prison authorities. He felt even more awkward handling money and buying a train ticket to the next town. The attendant must have known he was dealing with an ex-convict, for he was surly and unhelpful. And when he went out onto the platform, McConnell was sure everyone was looking at him. Self-conscious, lowering his eyes to his feet, he walked to the far end of the station, waiting for the train, which the attendant had said should be arriving soon.

McConnell kept sending anxious glances up the track, wanting to leave this place and all its harsh memories behind. It was just as the train whistle sounded in the distance that he saw a man standing nearby, staring at him. No, not staring, watching. As McConnell glared at him, the man looked quickly away. He was in his late thirties, and dressed all in black, from the brim of his hat to the tips of his boots, even his shirt was black. McConnell could feel the man's eyes boring into him.

Stop it, he said to himself. This was stupid. He had to stop imagining that people were taking special notice of him. Why should they be? They were probably quite used to ex-prisoners on the station platform. Why should a complete stranger be watching him?

He mustn't brood over what was now the past; he had to think about the future instead. It was a fine Spring morning. The sun was shining, the sky almost cloudless, blossom appearing on the trees.

He should have been happy. After ten long years he was free. No more being locked up in a tiny cell, no more guards telling him what to do, no more brutality or dull boredom day after day. No more prison food.

But even freedom could be a problem to someone with hardly any money, no expectations and no idea of what to do with a future that yawned frighteningly wide in front of him.

McConnell leant against the bar and picked up the glass of beer. Staring at it for a moment, he then took a slow sip, savouring its taste. He debated on whether or not to drink it down in one gulp and order another. And decided against it. He couldn't afford such extravagence.

Aware of the bartender, who this early in the evening wasn't exactly busy, hovering nearby, he said, 'Any work around here, mister?'

'Mebbe,' the bartender replied non-committedly. 'But you might have trouble getting a job.'

'Why?'

'You're just out of prison ain't you?'

Nervously touching the tight collar of the shirt he'd been given to wear, McConnell stared at his reflection in the fly blown mirror over the bar. He was thirty-one and looked older, especially as his face was so thin, with dark circles under the eyes. His dark brown hair was cut prison short.

'Is it that obvious?'

The bartender shrugged. 'Not particularly. Most of the ex-convicts from the prison come through the town and they usually head straight here for a drink or two, maybe even a whore. Mostly I can recognise 'em.'

Talking of whores, McConnell had been very aware of the two or three women flitting around the room. Aware too of their low-cut blouses and short skirts showing trim ankles. God, but it had been a long time since he'd enjoyed a woman's

company. And God it was going to be even longer.
No way had he enough cash to take a whore to bed
and no way was one of them going to give their
favours for free, especially to a just released
prisoner with no prospects.

'I've served my time,' he said a bit sulkily. 'I don't
want any trouble.'

'What were you in for?'

'Bank robbery.'

The bartender gave a silent whistle. 'You don't
look the type.'

'I was persuaded.' McConnell's eyes clouded
over with sullen remembrance.

'Well, son, iffen I was you I wouldn't make any
secret of my past. You'll be found out in the end
and then it'll look even worse. Most people are
willing to forget a man's mistakes but they ain't so
eager to forgive his lies. But that don't necessarily
go for around here. You might want to go straight,
you might be honest but it's a sad fact that a helluva
lot of just released men seem to do all they can to
head right back to jail. Most of the folks in town
have been cheated in one way or another and
they're getting mighty fed up with it. You'd do
better to go on aways before you try your luck.
What did you do before you got put away? Besides
rob banks I mean.'

'I grew up on a farm.'

The bartender grinned knowledgeably. 'I suppose you left it because at the time it appeared like
damn hard work for little reward? But if you look
at it now you'll perhaps realize it wasn't nearly so
hard as being in prison.'

Well that was for sure, McConnell thought. And
his folks didn't live all that far away. According to

his mother's latest painfully spelled letter, his two brothers were now married with children and places of their own, but his father was still farming the land Andrew had grown up on. But how could he go home? He daren't. He feared everyone's reaction on his arrival.

'Where you bedded down?' the bartender broke in on his thoughts.

'In the livery. The owner said it'd be all right for a couple of nights.'

'Tomorrow morning you come on back here and I'll see about getting you a free lunch. You look like you could do with some feeding up.'

'Thanks.'

A group of men came in and the bartender moved away to serve them. McConnell picked up his still almost full glass of beer and turned around, looking at the saloon and its occupants. It wasn't much of a place, being small and smelly, but filling up as it now was, it was full of noise and laughter: men enjoying themselves drinking, smoking, talking to the girls, others settling down in the corner for a game of poker.

It reminded him with a sharp twist of his heart of all that he'd missed out on. In his youth, his home town saloon was nothing like this, allowing neither gambling nor whores. And although Ray had promised him the time of his life, they'd usually been too busy running from the law to bother about saloons and brothels.

And Christ he'd only been twenty when he got caught and just turned twenty-one, when his life should have been beginning, when he was sentenced to ten years in prison. He remembered breaking down and crying when Judge Neely delivered the sentence. And the judge had sternly told him to count his blessings, because he was getting off lightly on account of his youth and the fact he hadn't been in trouble before.

Ray had a lot to answer for. But, in fairness, it hadn't been all his fault. No-one had forced McConnell to leave the drudgery of the farm and embark on an exciting life of crime. The double-cross had been all Ray's though.

McConnell swallowed some more of his beer. He didn't have enough money to indulge in revenge. Instead he had to forget about Ray Vaughan and what had happened in the past, and think about himself and his future.

He stayed in the saloon for a while, taking in the sights and sounds. Still feeling uncomfortable amongst so many people, he sat in a corner where he could observe without being seen. When the beer was almost finished he tried to pretend it was going to last him for the rest of the evening. The bartender took pity on him.

'Here honey.' One of the girls put a full glass in front of him. 'Compliments of the house.'

She looked as if she wanted to linger but McConnell, longing for the company of a woman, just to sit and talk, had no idea of what to say. Disappointed, she wandered off.

It was getting late when he decided to go back to the livery stable to get some sleep. Tomorrow he would have to make up his mind about what he was going to do. It would probably be wise to take the bartender's advice and move on, quickly, before his money ran out. It wasn't going to be easy, the Warden had warned him that it wouldn't be, but he was determined not to go off the rails again. He'd do just about anything to earn some honest wages.

Nodding goodnight to the bartender, McConnell went out into the dark night, the sky full of stars. It had turned cold and he pulled his thin jacket further round him.

The livery stable was beyond several warehouses and barns. Once he crossed the intersection between the saloons and the business district, there were no street lights, the buildings all shut and locked up.

He was just passing an alley between two warehouses when, out of the corner of his eye, he glimpsed a movement: a deeper shadow against the black wall, the slither of noise. Before he could properly register it, someone dived out at him, strong arms wrapped themselves round him, and he was pulled backwards into the quiet black of the alley. McConnell yelled in fright but a hand, encased in a soft glove, slammed against his mouth, pushing his lips back against his teeth, cutting off sound.

Forcing paralysing fright from his mind, McConnell shoved at his attacker, but the man had him in such a grip that he could hardly move his arms, let alone free them. He kicked out, foot making contact with shin, but although the man grunted, he didn't let go. Instead he slammed a fist hard into Andrew's stomach. The air left McConnell's body with a whoosh and he bent forward gasping for breath. And at the same time saw the flash of a blade sweeping upwards aimed for his exposed neck.

Panting, McConnell managed somehow to bring an arm up. The knife sliced through jacket and shirt, cutting a long groove from wrist to elbow, causing him to yelp in shock and pain.

Falling backwards against the wall, mind telling him he was fighting for his life, he swallowed a wave of nausea and in desperation brought his knee up into the man's groin. It was his assailant's turn to scream and, as he staggered back, McConnell freed a hand and grabbed for the man's knife arm, catching hold of his wrist. He was punched round the jaw but took no notice, all his concentration centred on hanging onto the man. He was aware of blood pouring down his rapidly numbing arm, turning the ground slippery beneath his feet.

Whoever he was, the man was strong and pulled himself away from McConnell's hold. With a growl of triumph he brought the knife up to strike. McConnell dodged and the blade struck sparks off the wall. The man was knocked slightly off-balance by the force of his movement and Andrew seized the opportunity to slip away from the confining wall. Both hands grabbed for his attacker's arm again, one hand sliding down the knife blade, slicing open the palm. Grunting, finding the man's wrist again, as the man moved towards him, McConnell pushed hard.

The knife entered the man's body just below the heart. Gasping, mouth open in shock, he leaned forward, against McConnell, who instinctively put out a hand to support him. The dying man looked up at him, although it was too dark for McConnell to see anything, except the fading glint in his eyes.

As Andrew let go of man and knife, the man fell forward, face down in a trickle of McConnell's blood.

Gulping for air, McConnell stumbled out of the alley, holding his injured arm. He was shaking, aware, now it was over, that his heart was pounding so hard it felt like it would burst.

'Hold it right there,' a voice said from behind him and the barrel of a gun was jabbed into his back.

TWO

'Don't shoot,' McConnell said in an agonised whisper.

'Keep your hands where I can see 'em,' the voice ordered.

'I ain't armed.'

'No, he ain't.'

With relief, McConnell heard the bartender's voice. Slowly, and carefully, he turned his head. The man holding the gun on him wore a sheriff's star. Behind him was the bartender and several other citizens.

'Sheriff, over here,' someone called from the alley.

And the body of the dead man, knife still sticking from his chest, was dragged into the street.

With a start of surprise, McConnell recognized his attacker. It was the man all in black who had stood on the station platform, watching him.

The Sheriff stuck his gun deeper in McConnell's side. 'You kill him?'

'Only because the bastard was trying to kill me.'

'Who was he?'

'I don't know.'

'You expect me to believe that a man you don't know tried to kill you?'

'It's the truth.'

'Why would he do that?'

'Perhaps he wanted to rob me.'

'Pardon me for saying so but you don't exactly look like you're worth the attempt.'

'See.' McConnell held out his hand, palm upwards, revealing the cut down the middle. 'He tried to stab me. I'm goddamned bleeding to death here and all you can do is stand there asking me damnfool questions.'

'No need for that kind of talk son. Won't get you anywhere in the long run.'

'I think he's telling the truth,' the bartender spoke up. 'I saw that man dressed all in black in the saloon watching him. He left just afterwards and turned in the same direction.'

'All in black did you say?' The Sheriff asked sharply. He left McConnell and went to stare down at the corpse.

McConnell watched anxiously, not sure if the lawman believed him.

'Well I don't know who you are, mister, but while you don't appear up to much, you sure must be important to someone.' Before McConnell could ask the Sheriff what he meant, the man went on, 'One of you fetch the undertaker and you,' he nodded at the bartender, 'take Mr ...'

'McConnell.'

'Take Mr McConnell to the doc's and get his arm patched up or I'll have two corpses on my hands. And, Mr McConnell, it's too late to do any more tonight. But make sure you come and see me tomorrow. Don't do anything foolish like trying to leave town before I say you can. Understand?'

'Yeah,' McConnell agreed sulkily.

'Come on,' the bartender said, touching Andrew's good arm. As they walked away, he added, 'Don't worry. Sheriff Parker is a hard man but very fair. He'll not try to blame you for something you didn't do.'

McConnell wasn't any too sure about that. He didn't have a particularly favourable view of anyone involved with the law. But there wouldn't be any point in running away; to do so would make it seem he was guilty. And the Sheriff looked quite capable of shooting first and taking statements afterwards.

Anyway he was too tired. His arm and hand hurt and reaction and shock were setting in. All he wanted to do was see the doctor, go to the livery stable, curl up and fall asleep.

It was with great reluctance that the next morning McConnell went to the sheriff's office. The last time he'd been in a sheriff's office was when he'd been arrested for robbery. Now he had no idea of whether or not he was about to be arrested again, and this time for murder.

His arm was washed and bandaged, the doctor said the wound was neither deep nor serious.

'But it and that cut on your hand will hurt like hell until they heal,' he'd added.

He was about right in that, McConnell thought, his arm feeling stiff and awkward and his hand stinging every time he touched anything.

When he woke up, he'd washed face and neck in the livery's trough and combed his hair, trying to make himself as presentable as possible, in the hope that would make a favourable impression on the Sheriff. The previous evening, before collapsing in his makeshift bed, he'd tried to wash the blood off his shirt and now, when he put it on, it was still wet. He could do nothing about that nor the slashes in the sleeve of his jacket; he had no money to buy anything new.

Sheriff Parker was alone in the office as McConnell went in. He indicated for Andrew to sit opposite him, which he did, feeling most uncomfortable. At least Parker hadn't got the handcuffs or the key to a cell ready. Even so he didn't look very happy.

'You know, Mr McConnell, I don't like murder on the streets of my town, whatever the reason. It doesn't look good.'

'It wasn't my fault.'

'Oh but I think you were to blame.'

'I was attacked,' McConnell went on with a note of desperation in his voice. 'All I did was defend myself. You can't blame me for doing that.'

'Have you managed to come up with any good reason why, if you're telling the truth, this man attacked you?'

'No I ain't. Look Sheriff I don't know if you know it or not but I only got out of prison yesterday ...' God, was it only yesterday? So much had happened, it seemed a lot longer. ' ... unless it was attempted robbery I ain't had time to annoy anyone that much they'd want to knife me.'

Smugly, Sheriff Parker nodded his head as if to acknowledge the fact that he might have guessed McConnell was an ex-convict. 'Oh no, Mr McConnell, it wasn't attempted robbery.'

'How do you know?'

'Believe me.'

'Then perhaps he just didn't like my goddamned face.' McConnell was getting angry at the man's snide comments.

'That explanation don't fit either. You see that man you killed last night was none other than Black Jack Pemberton. So called, of course, because he wears, or rather wore, nothing but black.' Sheriff Parker looked at him expectantly but the name meant nothing to McConnell, who shook his head in bewilderment.

'Black Jack Pemberton is, was, a well known hired killer. He usually worked in Wyoming or Montana, where he hid out amongst others of his own kind and was safe from the law. There's no way he would have come all the way down here to Colorado just to kill a stranger, unless he was hired to do so. He does, did, kill people for sport but only if he had a grudge against them. Yet you say you didn't know him?'

'No, I didn't.'

'How long were you in prison?'

'Ten years.'

'Hmm.' Sheriff Parker pulled at his long nose. 'Then perhaps you're right. Black Jack has never been in prison. It appears Mr McConnell that, despite your declaration that you ain't got any enemies, someone doesn't like you enough to have paid Black Jack to kill you. Any ideas as to who or why?'

Ray Vaughan! It had to be!

'No,' McConnell lied.

'Well I ain't so sure about that but it's your problem and I guess you won't be staying around here long enough for it to matter to me.'

There was a veiled threat in the Sheriff's voice and McConnell said, 'I'm moving on as soon as I can.'

'Good. I really don't like your sort coming round here causing trouble.'

McConnell glared at him sulkily but said nothing. There was nothing much he could say.

The Sheriff went on, 'However before you go you'd better take this note down to the bank and collect your reward.'

'Reward?'

'Yeah. There was a reward out for Black Jack. Dead or alive.'

'How much?'

'Five hundred dollars.'

McConnell burst out laughing. It looked as if good old Ray had done him one real big favour!

Five hundred dollars.

It was more money than McConnell had seen in his whole life before; except for that from the bank robbery and that hardly counted, especially as he'd had his hands on it for so short a time. He was rich! Well, while he might not be exactly rich, it at least gave him a certain amount of freedom to do what he wanted.

He went on a shopping spree.

He bought a pair of jeans, leather boots, a vest, thick jacket because the Colorado nights were still cold, and a couple of spare shirts: clothes he felt comfortable in.

And a revolver, a rifle and plenty of ammunition for both.

Then he treated his friendly bartender to a meal in one of the cafes and spent the afternoon in bed with a saloon whore. Once in the room with her, McConnell suffered from a fit of embarrassment, but she didn't seem to mind the fact that he was badly out of practice, and given encouragement he started to make up for lost time.

Sipping beer back down in the saloon, he then allowed his thoughts to drift to Ray Vaughan.

The bastard.

The Sheriff was right. Black Jack Pemberton wouldn't come all this way merely to kill a stranger. And if he'd been hired to kill someone else, why follow McConnell all the way from the railroad station? No, McConnell was the intended victim all right, and the only person with any reason to pay to have him killed was Ray Vaughan. Oh, he'd made enemies in prison but none bad enough they were that desperate to get rid of him.

All the while McConnell had been in jail plotting revenge, Ray, scared that Andrew would come looking for him, was, in turn, plotting what he was going to do about him. Not content with stealing ten years from him, Ray now wanted to steal his life as well. He must have a helluva lot to lose. But however much that was, when it came to it, Ray had a nerve. Because, after all, it was McConnell who had already lost quite a lot.

And Vaughan had been wrong. The thoughts of vengeance, that had kept McConnell going for ten years, had mostly disappeared. It was different now.

Someone like Ray wouldn't give up. Another killer would come along. McConnell's luck had held up against Black Jack; he couldn't expect it to do so again.

The only thing to do was find Ray Vaughan before Vaughan found him.

But how? Where was he now?

It was no use asking Sheriff Parker for help. Not only did McConnell mistrust the law, but why should the Sheriff show any interest in Andrew's problems? Besides he had made it clear he hadn't got any time for an ex-convict who knifed people on his streets, whatever the provocation. Probably the only reason he hadn't thrown McConnell into jail was because the death of someone like Black Jack Pemberton would do him good come the next election.

Thinking of the dead killer, McConnell grinned. Perhaps the answer to Vaughan's whereabouts lay with Black Jack.

The undertaker's was conveniently situated next door to the doctor's. While a light burned in the doctor's parlour, the undertaker's was all in darkness. To save people's sensibilities, the entrance was at the back.

McConnell looked round before going up the side. He didn't want to be caught. It was raining. Most people were indoors. No one was about. Naturally the door was shut and locked but next to it was a window and this was slightly open. When he pushed it, it creaked in protest, but the rain beating on the mortuary's tin roof drowned out all other noise.

The window was narrow but McConnell had gained little weight in prison and he slipped through it quite easily, landing in the hallway beyond. The place was quiet. Deathly quiet, he thought, shuddering at his own joke.

Holding his breath and walking on tiptoe, which seemed the right thing to do even though no one was about who could hear him, McConnell opened the door in front of him. A kitchen. But the next one led to the room at the back where the bodies were laid out.

There was only one. It lay on the table in the

middle, covered with a sheet.

McConnell lifted the sheet. Yes, it was Black Jack Pemberton. Naked. Black Jack's clothes, all in black of course, were hanging from hooks on the wall, boots neatly placed below them.

Andrew began to go through the pockets. At first there was nothing. Then his fingers delved into an inside pocket of the coat and there he found a piece of paper.

It was an empty envelope addressed to Mr Pemberton at Deer Flats, Wyoming.

That was all the information McConnell needed. He beat a quick exit from the undertaker's and the forever silent body of Black Jack Pemberton.

THREE

Mary Packman, or Moffat as she was now, lived on the outskirts of Colorado Springs.

McConnell sat on his hired horse, under the shelter of a dripping oak tree, staring across at her house. Trying to get up the courage to go and see her but thinking that he'd probably ride away without doing so.

It was a small but neat house with a covered porch in front, a tiled roof and a garden with a white picket fence. A child's swing stood in one corner, a hoop lying near the porch steps.

McConnell sighed heavily and was about to turn his horse's head, when the door opened and a woman came out. She was his age, plumper than he remembered, wearing her hair fixed up in a plain style that suited her just as much as the pretty curls she'd once had. She spoke to someone behind her and a girl of about five came out, circled her mother and ran out into the garden.

It had stopped raining and the woman, Mary, followed the girl down off the porch and walked to where the hoop was, stooping to pick it up. As she straightened, she saw McConnell watching her and raised a hand to her mouth, half in fright as if wondering what a man was doing there. She said

25

something to the little girl, who immediately went inside.

Slowly Mary took a step forward, lowering her arm and McConnell saw the suddenly rigid lines of her body. She'd recognized him just as he recognized her. It was too late to leave. He jigged the horse forward up to the gate in the fence and dismounted. 'Hallo Mary.'

'Oh Andy, Andy, it is you.' Mary said and turned away, beginning to weep.

'Don't cry, please.' McConnell walked up to her, standing close, but careful not to touch her. 'It's all right. I'm out of prison now. I ain't going back. It's all right.'

Mary faced him. 'But you're so thin. Look at you. What did they do to you in that dreadful place? And your hand is all bandaged.'

'It's nothing.' McConnell made light of the knife wound, not telling her how much it hurt.

He followed her indoors, through a dimly lit hall, to a tidy kitchen. Gleaming copper pans hung from hooks in the ceiling, the table was scrubbed pine. A door opened onto a flagged yard.

The girl and a chubby boy of three had come running to see who the visitor was and now stood watching him, thumbs in mouths.

'Andy these are my children! Martha Ann and George Andrew.'

'You named him after me?'

'Now you two, go outside and play. And be quiet.'

'Yes Mama.' Hand in hand the two children skipped out into the yard, glad to leave their suddenly sad-eyed mother.

'Sit down. There's beef stew heating up on the stove. Would you like some?'

'Only if it ain't going to get you into trouble.'

Mary smiled weakly. 'My husband knows all about you. He won't want to meet you but he'll understand why you came to see me. I'm so sorry.'

'What for?'

'Not waiting for you. I meant to, really I did. Then I met George. He made me laugh again. It seemed such a long time since I'd laughed. Oh, Andy, why did you do it? Life on the farm wasn't that bad was it?'

'Of course it wasn't. But it seemed like it was to a twenty year old who'd seen nothing of life. Ray seemed to offer so much more. Then once I'd started out with him there was no way I could stop even if I'd wanted to. I didn't think it would make any difference to us. It was a helluva shock when I found out your parents had forbidden you to speak to me.'

'I wouldn't have taken any notice of what they said.'

'I know. And I meant to come back to you. I really believed I could.'

They were both silent for a while, remembering how Mary had begged him not to go off with Ray. And then how she had bravely made the long journey all alone to the town where McConnell was waiting in jail for his trial, defying her parents to do so. The Sheriff hadn't allowed them to touch and they had stood either side of the cell bars, aching for one another, swearing undying love.

Once he'd gone to the penitentiary, Mary had written several times, expressing her love for him, but gradually the letters changed. Unable to bear her parents' condemnation of both him and her, she had moved away to Colorado Springs. Taken a teaching job. Met a bank clerk of all things. And finally that she was going to marry George Moffat.

McConnell no longer loved her, except as a memory. How could he? He hadn't seen her in ten years and this happily married woman of thirty, mother to two children, was very different to the naive farm girl of nineteen he'd made love to in her father's barn, and then up and left. And why the hell had he done that? For excitement? Adventure? God. He could have been with her these last ten years, enjoying her company, loving her, living a pleasant normal life.

'I ain't going to pretend I wasn't upset when I got your letter. I was pretty shook up by it but I soon came to realize it was the right thing for you to do. You had your whole life in front of you. I couldn't expect you to wait for me all that time and when I got out what could I offer you? Nothing like this,' McConnell indicated the kitchen. 'Nothing like those kids out there.'

'They're good children. And George is a good husband. I love him very much. And now you'll have the chance to find someone of your own.'

'It won't be a decent girl, Mary. What decent girl would want an ex-convict, a bank robber, for a husband?'

'You've served your time. You can put all that behind you.'

'I wish it were that easy. Look at me. Listen to me. I've been careful of my language in front of you but normally I swear all the time. I ain't, haven't, lived in the ordinary world for ten years, I don't know how to behave in it any more.'

'Before, you were an ordinary decent boy, it shouldn't be so hard to become a decent man.'

McConnell shook his head, and Mary reached over, squeezing his hand. 'What did they do to you in prison?' She repeated her earlier question that McConnell hadn't answered.

'It wasn't so bad, not once I stopped fighting it.'

But at first, betrayed, full of impotent anger, McConnell had fought it all. It hadn't done him any good. All it had done was get him beaten up by the guards and by his fellow prisoners, and thrown into the hole to endure solitary confinement through the heat of the days and the freezing cold nights. One of the older guards, taking pity on him, had warned him that he had no choice but to serve his sentence. The best way was to accept it, get on with it. Otherwise he was going to get himself killed.

Reluctantly McConnell took the advice. He'd done the work given him, eaten the bad food without complaint, put up with the boredom.

And slowly day after long day, ten years had come and gone.

'I still don't see why you were given such a long sentence.' Mary's eyes were full of tears again. 'You didn't deserve it.'

'Yeah, I did. I did wrong. I'd have probably done worse if I hadn't gotten caught.'

'You don't know that. And you wouldn't have done any of it, or got caught, if it hadn't been for Ray Vaughan.' Mary added bitterly.

McConnell took a deep breath. 'Did Ray ever get in touch with you? Do you know where he went?'

'No. I tried to find out what happened to him but he left the area and never came back. He wouldn't have dared show his face around me or your family. I did hear that he changed his name and started up a ranch somewhere. But that could have been just a rumour. Andy,' she cried, suddenly realizing what his questions might mean, 'you're not going after him are you?'

'I must.'

'You're going to shoot him for what he did, aren't you?'

'No, I want to talk to him is all.' McConnell knew that was true. Despite being exposed to the harshness of prison life, and mixing with all sorts of criminals, he wasn't a killer; he couldn't just walk up to Ray and shoot him, however much Ray deserved it. 'I've got to try and sort things out between us.'

'You'll only get hurt again.'

'That's a chance I'll have to take.' He couldn't tell her about Black Jack Pemberton. She was upset enough without finding out that he'd almost been stabbed to death.

'Well just remember, Andy, that if he's used that stolen money wisely, he's probably considered an honest, decent man. You're an ex-convict. The law will be on his side.'

'It ain't something I'm likely to forget.'

'I think you'd better go now. George will be home soon.'

'All right.' He stood up. She was standing next to him and awkwardly he kissed her on the cheek.

There were no more words between them as he went outside and got on his horse. When he reached the corner of the road he stopped and looked back.

Mary still stood on the porch, watching him, her two children clinging to her skirts. She raised a hand to wave goodbye.

McConnell turned away. He knew he'd never see her again.

FOUR

Staring down at the porch from the bedroom window, Julie Vernon watched her husband pace backwards and forwards. He was staring at the track leading into town. Early that morning he had sent the foreman into Medicine Creek and now, with evening shadows lengthening across the ground, he was waiting for Tony Lane's return.

Julie didn't know what Lane's errand had been. Vernon rarely discussed anything with her, let alone ranch business. That it was something important was obvious from his mood all day. He'd been even more impatient and bad-tempered than usual. Julie had wisely kept out of his way, only meeting him at the midday meal. Then she had kept quiet, eyes lowered to the plate, not saying or doing anything that might turn that impatience and bad temper on her.

With a heavy sigh, Julie stepped back from the window, catching sight of herself in the fancy mirror hanging on the bedroom wall.

She was short and slightly plump, with fair hair waving down to her shoulders. Her clothes were the best her husband's money could buy. Not that he was a generous provider. But he liked to show her off and it would have been bad for his image if

she didn't dress well and if others knew how mean
he really was. She was still pretty but since her
marriage to Roy Vernon two years ago, lines of
worry and unhappiness round her light brown eyes
were quickly destroying her looks.

Where had it all gone wrong? Why? She had
intended it should all be so perfect.

Julie had fancied herself in love with Roy
Vernon almost as soon as he'd appeared in
Medicine Creek, ten years ago. With his black hair,
dark eyes and fashionable clothes, he was
handsome, charming and sophisticated. Several
years older than her, he was so unlike any of the
other boys or young men of sixteen year old Julie's
limited acquaintance, to whom her thoughts were
beginning to turn.

Vernon was also rich and said he was from the
East and had come to Wyoming looking for a ranch
to buy with money from a legacy. A small deserted
place outside of town had proved attractive; mostly
because there was plenty of spare land roundabout
which could be taken over for grazing. The
Rocking V was born and for eight years Vernon
worked hard to build the ranch up, until he could
sit back and be satisfied that he was both rich and a
success.

In those eight years, Julie had matured from a
young girl into a woman, who was still in love with
him. She danced with him at barn dances, shared
picnics at church socials, even visited him several
times at his ranch. She had dismissed the quick
kisses and hasty fumbles of her other suitors and
allowed herself to be seduced by Vernon's slow and
careful courting. She was flattered he wanted her
when surely someone so elegant and personable

could have had the pick of any girl, even someone from back East.

When he asked her to marry him, she agreed at once and the marriage had taken place soon after.

It hadn't been long before Julie realized that, in a wife, Vernon didn't want a partner, he wanted a decoration. She could have fought against that, perhaps even put up with it. But then she found that, even worse, he was a bully.

Her marriage was a dreadful mistake. Her love had quickly died in an atmosphere of mistrust, meanness and cruelty, leaving her feeling nothing for him but contempt.

But how could she admit it? How could she admit to others what it was so hard to admit to herself: that she'd been completely wrong about him? She had lived in Medicine Creek all her life and couldn't face the disgrace that would follow if she left him. Even worse if Bart was to find out about some of the things Vernon had done to her, marshal or not, he'd come gunning for him.

The sound of hoofbeats from outside disturbed Julie's unhappy thoughts. She crossed back to the window. A horse and rider was rapidly approaching the house.

Tony Lane. And why Roy felt it necessary to employ people like Lane, and those other two who were always with him, Julie didn't know. She had been born and raised in the West and knew a bad man when she saw one. And Lane, with his thick lips and greedy eyes, was surely more bad man than cowpuncher. He frightened her. She didn't like the way he looked at her or the way he always hung around the house when her husband wasn't there. But Roy was so unreasonably jealous she didn't dare say anything, because she feared Roy would accuse her of encouraging the foreman, and it would result in Lane getting shot and herself hurt.

'At last!' Vernon said as Tony Lane pulled his horse to a halt.

Lane grimaced. Quite how his boss had expected him to make the journey any quicker was beyond him. It was a good job Vernon paid well or he'd have left a long time ago. As annoyingly slowly as possible, he dismounted, banging dust from his jacket. 'Got back as soon as I could.'

'Yeah, yeah,' Vernon interrupted impatiently. 'Well?'

'Weren't anyone on the stage like you described, boss.'

'Goddammit! Are you sure?'

'Sure I am.' Lane tried not to grin, enjoying Vernon's discomfiture. He'd be willing to do anything for the man, or rather the man's money; that didn't mean he had to like him.

Vernon stared across at the foothills, mauvey pink where the sun shone on their peaks, the valleys in gathering dusk. 'Something's gone wrong. It must have done.'

'It just might be he doesn't want to come here.'

'No! I was most specific that I wanted evidence of the kill! Someone like Pemberton wouldn't forego the rest of his payment. If he'd done it he'd have been here now, flourishing his proof and claiming his money. His work depends on reliability. He wouldn't accept and pocket half the money and not do the job. That would be bad for future business.'

'Perhaps he hasn't found the opportunity to kill this McConnell yet.'

Vernon bestowed a look of pity on his foreman. 'I wanted it done as soon as possible. That was part of the deal.'

Lane wasn't too sorry that apparently, for some reason or the other, the famous killer, Black Jack Pemberton, had failed in his latest assignment. He had no idea how much his boss had been willing to pay the man. It was obviously a lot more than he paid his foreman.

Lane had asked to be given the chance to go after Andrew McConnell himself. Vernon was taking no chances and said no. Now it seemed his foolproof scheme had failed, and McConnell might be alive and coming for him after all.

'You, Franklin and Poynton keep your eyes open for any strangers. Tell the other hands as well. Make them think this man is out to destroy me because he's a rustler I had put away. Cowhands don't like rustlers.'

Vernon watched his foreman lead his horse to the stables. He knew very well Lane didn't like him. Most people who really knew him didn't. But Lane was greedy, willing to do anything for money. Vernon knew all about the power of money, he always had.

He also knew about fear. Ten years had come and gone and now that stupid sonofabitch McConnell was out of jail and able to inflict the revenge he'd sworn to carry out. Of course, Vernon had long since come up to Wyoming and changed both his name and his lifestyle. It was likely that McConnell, who had no brains, would spend years looking and never find him; but no way was Vernon going to give up his ranch and the life he enjoyed, not if he could help it.

He liked the respect given to him everywhere he went, and now there was the possibility that come the next elections he'd be voted in as Mayor. Besides, although he wouldn't say it even to himself, he was a coward and the idea of McConnell out there gunning for him was enough to send him into a cold sweat panic. He couldn't live with the constant fear that at any moment a bullet might strike him in the back.

A noise behind him caused him to swing round. Julie stood in the doorway. How much had she heard? He stroked his clipped black moustache and took a step towards her. 'How long were you there? Did you hear what me and Lane were talking about?' He grabbed her shoulders, shaking her.

'No.' Julie pulled away. 'I only came to tell you that dinner is almost ready. Honestly Roy whatever is the matter with you?'

Vernon said, 'Nothing.' And stalked by her into the house. He stopped to turn and point a finger at her. 'Just remember who you're married to.'

'I'm unlikely to forget.'

'And remember you owe me your loyalty.'

'Really, Roy, I don't know what you're talking about.'

Dennis Franklin and Mal Poynton both looked up to Tony Lane. In their early twenties, the two of them had been friends for some time.

Franklin was trying to grow a beard to make up for the fact that he looked even younger than he was. He had baby blue eyes, ginger hair and a pale complexion that burnt in the sun. Poynton was two years older, short but stocky with long brown hair.

He had once been a promising wrangler but lazyness had prompted him to take an easier course through life.

'So, if we see someone we don't like the looks of, Mr Vernon wants us to shoot him then find out who he is,' Lane said, pouring whisky for all three of them.

They were sitting in the two-room shack specially built for the foreman, away from the other cowhands in the bunkhouse.

Franklin grinned. Although he'd never been in a fight, he considered himself good with guns, and practised every day with the two Colt 45s he always wore in specially decorated holsters. Now perhaps here at last he would have his chance at killing someone.

Poynton was more cautious. 'Suppose the stranger we kill is innocent?'

'Then Vernon says he'll pay us to keep it quiet. And he'll pay us a good bonus if we do kill the right one.' Lane grinned. 'We can't lose.'

'Who is this McConnell that the boss wants him dead so bad? What's he done?'

Lane shrugged. He had no idea but whatever it was had spooked Vernon real bad. 'Vernon says that he was responsible for sending him to prison and that McConnell swore vengeance.'

'You don't believe him?' Franklin asked.

'Oh I believe that. What I don't believe is that Vernon is lily white pure with nothing to hide. If that was true then he would have gone to the law for help, not employed you two. Certainly not paid out good money to hire a killer. Whatever happened, Vernon is shit scared, that much I do know.'

'Let's hope McConnell does show up,' Poynton said. 'Then we can kill him, get our money and move on.' He didn't like Roy Vernon any more than Lane did; more particularly he didn't like the way Vernon treated his wife.

'I might come with you,' Lane said. 'I'm fed up with the pompous bastard and his superior attitude.' He too was thinking of Julie Vernon; but not in Poynton's respectful manner. It might just be that when he left he'd take pretty Mrs Vernon with him. She'd probably seize the chance to escape her husband. And if she didn't she could always be persuaded, forcibly if necessary.

FIVE

McConnell decided to take the stage to Deer Flats where Black Jack Pemberton had once lived. It would be quicker and more comfortable than riding across a country he didn't know. Apart from a motherly looking woman and a drummer, he was the only passenger. Securing a window seat, he pulled his hat down over his eyes, making it obvious that he didn't wish to join in any conversation.

Gradually, with the sun shining in on him and the rhythmic jolting of the carriage, his eyes closed. His arm had hurt the night before so he hadn't slept much and now he was tired.

He'd just turned twenty and was working on his father's farm, as he had done all his life, when Ray Vaughan rode up. He'd wanted a drink of water for both himself and his tired horse.

Andrew didn't know many people. Those he did were all like himself and his family: mostly poor farmers, who spent all their lives working and any leisure talking about work.

The slightly older Ray, with his dashing good looks, ready smile and store-bought clothes, was completely different. Almost like one of the heroes out of the dime novels Andrew was forbidden to read.

39

That evening Andrew rode the old mule into town and went into the saloon where he'd found Ray drinking whisky and telling tall tales. Eventually everyone else drifted away, leaving the two young men on their own.

'Have a whisky on me.'

'All right.' Although he'd only ever drunk beer before, Andrew agreed, not wanting to lose face. He sipped at the strange liquor, not particularly liking the taste but not willing to admit it. 'Are you staying round here long?'

'Not likely,' Ray laughed. 'This town ain't for the likes of me. It's much too quiet and respectable. I'm surprised someone like you is content to stay here.'

Andrew went red. He'd thought about leaving lots of times but never got up the courage to do so.

'I suppose you like working on a farm?'

'Not specially. It's all I know how to do.'

'You can always learn a new trade. Have you got a girl?'

'Yes.' Andrew went red again, thinking of Mary, and what her father would do to him if he knew what Andrew had done to Mary in the barn.

'Does she want you to remain a farmer forever more?'

'We haven't discussed it. If I left she'd come with me,' Andrew added with a certainty he didn't altogether feel. 'Anyway I'm not going.'

'You ought to. You could do so much better for yourself. Why not come with me? Of course,' Ray looked round the saloon to make sure they weren't overheard, 'you'd have to be willing to travel most of the time. I daren't stay in any one place too long.'

'Why not?'

'I'm wanted by the law!'

Andrew gaped at him. 'You're joshing me.'

'No, I ain't. I've got a price on my head. I robbed a trader's store back in Denver and nearly got caught. They don't know my name but they've got my description sure enough.'

'Is there a wanted poster out on you?' Andrew knew all about such things from the exciting stories he read about Jesse James.

'I ain't sure. I didn't stay in Denver long enough to find out. I hightailed it out quick.'

He even talked like a dime novel desperado!

'Are you a robber then?'

'Sort of,' Ray replied vaguely. 'You see, like you, I come from a small town but unlike you I never intended to stay there and do what my folks said. I aim to be rich and people like us can't get rich by working for others. So I decided to go into business for myself.'

'By stealing from people?'

'Only from those richer than me. I've already got more money in a couple of months than I'd ever seen before in twenty-four years. Here.' Proudly, he pulled out a purse and showed Andrew a pile of silver dollars, which caused Andrew to gape all over again.

'I don't know that I could rob anyone. It doesn't seem right.'

'It's easy,' Ray boasted.

'Supposing you got caught? You'd be put in jail.'

'I'd escape. Andy, why don't you come with me and try it for a while? If you don't like it you can always go home with no one being any the wiser.'

'What about Mary?'

'You can send for her when we get ourselves

settled. Just think, you'd have something far more
to offer her than being the wife of a dirt scrabble
sodbuster. Maybe you could live in San Francisco.
Even go East. Wouldn't you like to see something
of the world? Wouldn't you like to show Mary a
good time?'

Of course he would. Andrew's wants and desires
got the better of his good sense. Why shouldn't he
have something for himself for once? What had he,
up till now? Hand-me-down clothes from his two
brothers; dead baby sisters that broke his mother's
heart; beatings from his father. Poverty and
sometimes near starvation when a winter was
particularly harsh. Ray Vaughan offered him the
way out.

Andrew took it.

He bid a tearful goodbye to Mary, telling her
he'd write and that she could join him later on,
written a short but emotional letter to his mother,
packed a bag with his few belongings and sneaked
out of the house.

For a while, he didn't regret what he'd done.

Ray was a lively companion; happy-go-lucky,
freedom loving but careful too so there didn't seem
much chance that they'd ever be caught. On the
road they met others like themselves who accepted
Andrew McConnell, the farmboy, and made him
welcome. It was thrilling – a wild tale come true!

Once, when the law was far behind them, there
was even a visit to a brothel, which made Andrew's
eyes almost pop out of his head, what with the
pictures on the wall and the statues in the corners.
At first he felt uneasy, being unfaithful to his
faithful Mary, but the girl Ray picked out for him
was tiny and pretty with long dark hair and a

slender figure. Andrew didn't like to say no in case he was open to ridicule; seeing the girl he didn't want to say no.

Then one day Ray said, 'We've robbed all the places round here, successfully too, it's time we went up in the world.'

'What, give up you mean?' Andrew was disappointed. It felt good to have more money than he could spend in his pocket. Money he could use for luxuries not just necessities.

'Of course not. We're doing too well for that. No, I meant we should rob a bank.'

'A bank?' Andrew paled. Country stores that stood all alone, usually tended by no more than one man, and where the law was often a day's ride away, was one thing. A bank in the middle of town with people all round and the law on the doorstep was quite another.

'I don't see why not. Hit 'em hard and quick when they ain't expecting it and we'll get away with it. Think of all that money. Easy pickings!'

For a while Andrew argued against the idea. He was no match for Ray's persuasive tongue. In the end he agreed.

Ray picked out what appeared to be an ideal place. A sleepy town with only one lawman, an ageing sheriff, but a large bank because it served a local mine.

'Come paydays extra guards are employed. Other times nobody much bothers. We'll be in and out before they know it.'

Dressed in white duster coats, just like their heroes, the James boys, they rode into the town. Like Ray predicted, not many people were around. Just a few women shopping and gossiping, some farmers down by the barn discussing the weather.

Even so Andrew's mouth felt dry, his hands sweaty as they dismounted outside the bank, tied their horses to the railing and stepped up onto the sidewalk. Everyone had to be watching them. They had to know what was about to happen. He wanted to turn back, get on his horse and ride out of town.

It was too late. Ray was already opening the door.

It was cool and dim inside the bank. The counter, protected by wooden railings, ran down one side. An ornate chandelier hung from the ceiling. In the rear was a large safe. There was only one customer, an elderly woman, while behind the counter were two male clerks and one female.

Ray and Andrew pulled out their guns and Ray said loudly, 'All right folks, do as we say and no one will get hurt.'

The customer stared and screamed and Ray told her to shut up and get over by the wall. 'You two,' he said to the male clerks, 'lay face down on the floor. And you young lady start filling these up.' He shoved two burlaps bags under the railing. 'Don't try anything stupid.'

Andrew risked a glance out of the window. Life was going on as normal. It seemed impossible that he was here inside a bank, robbing it, when he'd never even been inside a bank before. He hoped no one would see that he was shaking, gun barrel pointed at the clerks none too steady.

Soon the female clerk, watching Ray with scared eyes, had filled the bags.

'Now, open the safe.'

'I ... I can't.'

'What do you mean? Open it!'

'She's right sir,' one of her colleagues spoke up from the floor. 'It's on a time lock.'

'I don't goddamn believe you.' Ray strode around the counter, dragged the man up by his coat collar and shoved him towards the safe. He dug his revolver into the man's cheek. 'Open it goddamn you.'

'It's on a time lock. Honestly.'

'Come on, Ray, forget it,' Andrew said from over by the door.

'This is where all the money is. We've got goddamn peanuts otherwise. Christ man, do you want to get shot for your employer? He wouldn't get shot for you! Or do you want the little lady there hurt?' And Ray swung his gun towards the female clerk, who gave a cry of fright, and then quickly back on the man, digging the barrel into his skin.

'All ... all right,' the clerk stammered, reaching for his pocket.

'Careful!'

'The key, sir, the key.' With trembling hands the clerk inserted the key into the safe's lock and turned it.

Andrew gasped. The safe had five shelves and each shelf had stacks of money on it.

'Whooeee,' Ray whistled and shoved the man away, sending him sprawling to the floor. 'Come on, Andy, help me.'

Together the two young men filled up more bags with the money, filled their pockets, poked it under their hats. They were trying not to giggle at the same time, which would have sounded unprofessional. They were anxious too, to get away before anyone else came in.

'We're leaving now,' Ray said at last. 'You all get on the floor, you too ladies, and stay there for the count of one hundred, a slow one hundred mind. You ain't been hurt yet but poke your noses out of the door too soon and you'll sure as hell get 'em shot off!'

They'd hurried out of the bank, mounted their horses and spurred away.

Laughing they looked at one another, laughed again.

It had all been so easy!

Even so, Andrew was worried.

'What's wrong?'

'I don't think you should have threatened all those people, especially those two women.'

'Don't be stupid. It was necessary to frighten 'em to get 'em to do what I wanted. We wouldn't have got all this money if I hadn't. I wouldn't really have hurt anyone.'

'You wouldn't?'

'Course not.'

They couldn't hope to get away without some sort of pursuit. When they got to the foothills and stared back, the dust of a posse spiralled up into the air.

'Don't worry, Andy, they're miles behind. They'll never catch us up. Let's stop and count out the money.'

It came to a little over fifteen thousand dollars.

Andrew's eyes gleamed. With his share he could do whatever he wanted. He'd never have to go back to the farm! He was dreaming of all he could do with the money when Ray came up behind him. And knocked him out.

When Andrew came to, horses, money, Ray were all gone.

But he wasn't alone. Sitting across from him, gun pointed at him, was the local lawman. Being in his forties, he was much older than Andrew, but he was hardly the ageing decrepit Ray had described. Nor was there any shortage of men with him.

'Hallo there son,' the Sheriff said. 'Got yourself in a bit of bother ain't you?'

Andrew put a hand to his bruised head. What had happened? Where was Ray? There had to be some mistake. Then someone kicked him hard. He was dragged up and his hands cuffed behind him. The Sheriff didn't let the other men hit him too much because it was obvious he'd been double-crossed by his partner and had no idea of the man's or the money's whereabouts.

Come evening Andrew was hauled back into town, everyone coming out to watch. He was flung into a cell.

'I reckon you're going to jail for a long time,' the Sheriff warned him. 'Was it all worth it?'

McConnell woke up with a startled groan, not knowing where he was for a minute.

It was hot and, despite the glassless windows, the coach felt stuffy.

'Are you all right, dear?' The motherly woman looked at him in concern. 'You were dreaming. Nightmares by the sound of things.'

'It's nothing,' McConnell replied, his tongue feeling thick and furry in his mouth.

With his release from prison, he'd thought his nightmares were over. Thanks to Ray Vaughan, he had a whole new set of bad dreams to worry about.

SIX

The stagecoach only halted at Deer Flats if there were passengers to let down or pick up. Other times it went straight through, Deer Flats not being the sort of place any decent person would want to linger. The motherly woman lost all concern for McConnell when she saw he was getting out and gave him a loud sniff of disgust instead.

Several men on the saloon porch looked him over, saw nothing to worry about, and went back about their business.

McConnell carried his bag over to the cracked and broken sidewalk, and stared around.

Not that there was much to see. Just three saloons, a fancy brothel, a second-rate brothel, a dancehall and some cribs running down to the river. The only place not catering to gentlemen's entertainment was a general store. Besides gamblers, whores and hardened drinkers, most of the town's occupants were men on the run. Knowing that, for the most part the law left the place alone, they felt reasonably safe amongst their own kind.

McConnell went into the dark and low ceilinged store. A fat man, face covered with grey whiskers, stood behind a counter piled high with furs of every description. He stared suspiciously at Andrew, made him out to be another outlaw down on his luck, and didn't bother much about him.

'You got a room for the night?'

'Mebbe. You got the money to pay for it?'

'How much?'

'Fifty cents.'

'Yeah I got it.'

'Dinner's fifty cents more. Both in advance.'

McConnell handed over a dollar.

'You only staying one night then?'

'Probably.'

The storekeeper gave him a look. It said, oh well it's none of my business but it's a strange business all the same, and it had better not mean any harm for anybody, not while you're staying in my store.

'By the way I'm looking for a gent called Black Jack Pemberton.'

'Christ, mister,' the man breathed, suddenly scared.

'I was told he lives here in town.'

'What do you want him for?'

'Oh nothing much.'

'Look, mister, I don't know if you're a damnfool lawman, a fool gunslinger out to make his mark, or just a plain fool. But you're a stranger. I live in this Godforsaken place, I make a living in this store. I get on with folks. That's all. Black Jack might live here too but I don't want anything to do with him. He's bad news. What's more he ain't been around for several weeks now. Which is goddamned lucky for us.'

'Where does he normally hang out?' McConnell persisted in his questions.

'You go and speak to Joey.'

'Who's Joey?'

'His little brother. He owns the Lucky Night whorehouse.' The storekeeper turned away, the conversation at an end as far as he was concerned. 'I'll show you your room.' He was glad the stranger was only staying one night; the sooner he left the better.

McConnell wasn't surprised to find that the Lucky Night brothel was the second-rate one, situated across the weed strewn intersection, the whores' cribs the only buildings beyond it. He didn't want a girl but saw no alternative but to go inside in order to make the acquaintance of Joey Pemberton.

He need not have worried about having to pay for a girl. The Lucky Night only employed three soiled doves and they were all busy with customers – construction workers from the railroad some twenty miles north of town, which, in McConnell's mind, said something about the type of girl employed.

The brothel, no better inside than out with peeling paper, threadbare rugs and dust, also provided drinks, a honkytonk piano and gambling.

McConnell recognised Joey Pemberton as soon as he went in, even though he'd only seen Joey's elder brother on three occasions, and one of those was when the man was dead.

A young man of twenty or twenty-one, Joey was sitting at a corner table, playing cards with two others and getting the better of them if the pile of money in front of him was anything to go by. He was a dandy with slicked back dark hair, parted in the middle, a drooping moustache and fancy silver embroidered vest across which stretched a gold watch chain. McConnell was interested to see that, unlike his brother, Joey Pemberton wore not one item of black.

McConnell ordered a beer from the negro who also played the piano. Thinking it might seem strange as to why he had come in here rather than a saloon if a drink was all he needed, he said he might want a girl later on when one was free. Then he sat down on a springless sofa.

In order to ask Joey questions about Black Jack's final assignment, he obviously had to get him on his own, without any danger of being confronted by any bouncer the brothel might employ.

It was almost midnight before he got his chance.

Men had come and gone, girls had appeared and disappeared. The piano player bashed out jaunty tunes. And Joey had remained at the table, gambling. Finally, the two men with him gave in. They threw the cards down, got to their feet and dejectedly walked out, with not even enough money left to buy a drink, let alone a girl.

All three whores were in the room, chatting to potential customers. Picking up his winnings, Joey went over to the youngest and prettiest of the three – not that he had much choice, none of them being very young or very pretty – and pulled her to him. He put an arm round her waist and whispered something in her ear. Smiling, she nodded. And they left the room going down a side corridor by the bar.

At once McConnell stood up and wandered over to the end of the bar as casually fast as he could. Not that anyone took any notice of him. He got there just in time to see Joey and the girl disappear through a door. It must lead to Joey's private rooms. For every other transaction, the girls had taken the men upstairs.

At the end of the corridor was a small shadowed alcove with two other doors, both marked 'Private', in it. One led to a storeroom of sorts and heart beating fast, McConnell slipped inside, waiting where he hoped he couldn't be seen. From the room opposite came the sounds of giggles and groans, which made him smile.

He wondered about breaking in on their fun, but decided not to. Not that he had any scruples about disturbing Joey. But the girl might scream and alert others, or she might get hurt if Joey tried anything stupid. On the other hand, if it looked like she was going to stay in there for the night, he'd have to think again because he couldn't stay where he was for so long he risked discovery.

But it was only about fifteen minutes later when the door opened. McConnell pressed back into the shadows. The girl, doing up her blouse, didn't see him, but went back to the noise and light of the parlour to continue earning her living. Fearing that Joey might soon follow her, McConnell had no time to waste.

Drawing his revolver, he banged into the room. He grinned. Joey Pemberton was lying on the bed, stark naked, clothes and gunbelt placed neatly on a chair, well out of reach.

With an exclamation of surprise and fear, Joey sat upright. 'What the hell?'

'Quiet,' McConnell warned, shutting the door. 'Don't make a sound. I can shoot you before help can arrive.'

'Who the hell are you?' Joey asked, grabbing a sheet and pulling it across him.

'Never mind. Put your pants on. Then you're going to answer some questions.'

'What do you mean, questions? Who are you? Someone's husband? Or do you think I cheated you at cards? I don't know you, do I?'

'Be quiet. I ain't about to hurt you lessen you give me cause. Come here.' McConnell caught hold of the young man's arm, feeling him trembling. 'Now let's just sit down and talk.' He pulled forward two chairs and placed them side by side. Shoving Joey down into one he sat in the other, digging his gun into Joey's side.

'Please don't kill me, please. I'm sure I never hurt you on purpose.'

'Your brother's dead.' McConnell interrupted Joey's whimperings.

Joey looked at him, eyes widening. 'What, Jack?'

'Yeah, Black Jack, he's dead.'

'How do you know?'

'I'm Andrew McConnell, the one he was sent to kill.'

'Oh my God!' Joey began to babble in earnest now. 'Look I don't know anything abut Jack's business. I never liked what he did. I've never killed anyone. I run a brothel. I gamble and cheat and make love to every woman I can. But I don't go around killing people. You can ask anyone. You can't blame me for what my brother did.'

'For Chrissakes shut up!'

'I was scared of him. He made me shelter him. I didn't want to. Please.'

'I said shut up. I ain't going to take it out on you, not unless you force me to. Just listen for a moment. I want to know who hired Black Jack to kill me and where I can find the bastard.'

Joey ran a hand up and down his naked arm. 'Did you kill Jack? You must have done or you wouldn't be here.' He sighed but whether with relief or regret it was impossible to tell.

'Did he ever discuss his business with you?'

'Sometimes. Mostly because he knew I didn't want to hear.'

'Did he discuss me?'

'Sort of.'

'What does that mean? Come on, Joey. Perhaps you know I've just got out of prison. That means I'm used to violence and I ain't known for my gentle manners. Your brother tried to knife me. I killed him instead. That should tell you something about me. I'm out for revenge and I ain't got that much time or patience. You're the one in my way at the moment. Tell me what I want to know and I'll leave you alone. Otherwise ...' McConnell left the threat unsaid, mostly because he didn't have a suitable threat ready.

'Look, Mr McConnell, I'm only glad Jack is dead. I was always frightened that he would turn his knife on me. He used to beat me regularly and worse beat my girls as well.'

'In that case you shouldn't mind answering my questions.'

'I don't. The trouble is I don't know much.'

'Just tell me what you do know. And make it fast.' McConnell made his voice as harsh as he could, keeping Joey scared of him, so that he would tell the truth.

'I know he got a letter off the stage 'bout you. It said Jack was to wait around until you got out of prison and then he was to kill you as soon as he could. And he was offered a helluva lot of money.

Half now, the rest when he'd proved he done it.'

'Who hired him?'

'I don't know.'

'Try to remember.' McConnell poked Joey in the side with the gun barrel.

'No, Mr McConnell, that's the truth. Jack didn't know either.'

'Don't talk crap!'

'It's true. He often didn't know. All kinds of people hired Jack. Some were respectable and seemingly law-abiding. Can you imagine someone like that wanting someone else killed, and it being discovered because he'd signed his name to a letter hiring Jack? No, most of Jack's dealings were with those who wanted to remain anonymous.'

'So how was Black Jack meant to get the rest of his money?'

'He was to go to a place called Medicine Creek. There he'd be contacted and given the rest of the money once he'd proved you were dead.'

'Medicine Creek?'

'Yeah,' Joey nodded furiously. 'Yeah, Medicine Creek.'

SEVEN

Bart Wingate let himself out of the log cabin where he'd lived all his life. It had rained the night before and when he crossed the road he was up to his ankles in mud. No one else was yet around and his bootheels echoed loudly on the sidewalk in the early morning quiet. Although he didn't really need to, Bart liked getting up before dawn, when the mist rising from the river gave the buildings a glamour they didn't normally possess.

He could remember when Medicine Creek contained only a few houses and a couple of trading stores for the ranchers. His father had worked in one of those stores all his life. His one great hope had been that Bart would follow in his footsteps; not as a general clerk for someone else but owning a store of his own. It was what his parents scrimped and saved for. Bart had never been interested. He'd wanted to be a lawman ever since he could remember. As a child, he'd followed Marshal Hobbs everywhere around town, doubtless getting in the way but listening and learning too.

When he was sixteen he'd applied to become the Marshal's deputy. At first, his parents had refused to let him go, but Marshal Hobbs persuaded them that it was best to let Bart get it out of his system. He never had. He could still remember the pride he'd felt the day the deputy's star was pinned to his vest; a pride that had never left him.

Some four years ago, Hobbs decided he was getting too old for his position, especially as more and more people were arriving in the town and not all of them had respect for the law. He said he wanted to retire and live with his daughter and son-in-law over near Laramie. Hobbs had no hesitation in nominating his bright young deputy to take over. And the Town Council and the town voters had all agreed.

Now Bart was Marshal, in charge of his own deputies, doing what he felt was a good job, still getting fulfillment from what he did. It was time to think about getting married. And to that end Wingate had been busy taking out the cafe owner's daughter. Not only was she good looking, she was a good cook too. And Wingate was firmly of the opinion that in affairs of the heart, food was an important ingredient.

Although Medicine Creek was still relatively small, its main square now had shops selling all kinds of things, there were two banks. A hotel catered for the ranchers, two boarding houses for cowboys looking for work. The stagecoach called a couple of times a week. There was a church. Lately there'd been the additions of a school and a newspaper. Houses were spreading out over the surrounding hills.

There was even talk about the railroad putting in a spur line, something which several of the ranchers, led by Roy Vernon, were constantly demanding.

Speaking of Vernon, he was in town along with Julie and several of his men.

By now Wingate had reached his office. Inside, he opened up the shutters allowing a shaft of weak sunlight to streak across the cluttered room, and went over to the stove to start up some of the strong black coffee, with which he kept going through the day. A deputy was asleep in one of the cells, snoring loudly.

Waiting for the coffee to boil, Wingate went over to the window and stared out. Old Mr Simms from across the way was opening up his general store, sweeping the sidewalk in front as he had for the past twenty years. He gave Wingate a wave before going back inside.

Wingate didn't like Roy Vernon. He never had done. There was something about the man that wasn't quite right but evidently he was the only one to see it. And it wasn't just because Vernon had married Julie. He'd have preferred to see Julie married to a nice boy of her own age from Medicine Creek; not someone with Vernon's streak of ruthless ambition. But that had been her choice and he had never said anything to her about how he felt.

Neither did he like the men Vernon had hired lately, and who seemed to accompany him wherever he went. Tony Lane had caused trouble in the Bull's Head saloon last night, throwing his considerable weight around, until Wingate had to go over and tell him to shut it down or face a night in the cells. And all the while he'd been watched by Lane's two cohorts. Lane might look like a cowhand. Franklin and Poynton looked like trouble.

Wingate couldn't understand why Vernon had them out at the ranch. There seemed to be no reason for it; there was no trouble with rustlers or homesteaders whom Vernon might want to warn off with a show of force.

To Wingate's mind the situation needed keeping an eye on.

'Where have you been Roy?' Julie Vernon asked, sitting up in bed in the hotel room as her husband came through the door.

His cheeks were stubbly, eyes bloodshot. He looked dishevelled. 'Nowhere,' he snarled.

'Nowhere! It's six o'clock in the morning. You've been out all night. I was worried.'

'Here.' Vernon reached into his pocket and threw a handful of notes and coins on the bed. 'Buy yourself a dress. That'll stop your worries.'

It wouldn't, of course, but all the same Vernon was usually so mean that Julie wasn't about to refuse the money out of misplaced pride or anger. Instead she gathered it up carefully and put it on the table by the bed. He had surely made a mistake in the amount he'd thrown at her but she wasn't going to give any of it back. She'd spend it as soon as she could, before he changed his mind.

Vernon had obviously been drinking. He had probably also been to the brothel. Vernon had always visited the brothel when he came to Medicine Creek and he didn't see why a little thing like being married should stop him now.

The first time it had happened Julie had been dreadfully upset. She'd begged him not to go again. She was wasting her breath. Vernon said he always did what he wanted and she would have to

get used to it. Now she no longer minded, it saved
him bothering her. What she didn't like was the
fact that someone might find out. She couldn't
stand the thought of people's sympathy or
derision.

'What are you going to do today?' she asked as
Vernon began to undress, throwing his clothes on
the floor for someone else to pick up.

'I've got to see the parson about the church social
in a few weeks and later on there's a meeting to
discuss the railroad. I'll probably take the chance to
put forward a few ideas as to what I'm going to do
when I'm made Mayor of this backwater.'

'In that case you'd better get some sleep hadn't
you? You don't look much like a leader of men at
the moment.'

As Vernon flopped down in the bed beside her,
he said, 'I suppose you're going to see that brother
of yours?'

'Yes.' Julie knew that Roy would like to try and
forbid her from seeing Bart. He didn't dare. Bart
would come out to the ranch demanding to know
the reason why, and he wouldn't accept any lame
excuse such as Julie didn't want to see him.

'Well just be careful what you talk about.'

'Oh, go to sleep.'

'Hallo, Julie.' Wingate looked up from his desk and
smiled as his sister came into the office. 'How are
you?'

'All right, thanks.'

'Happy?'

'Of course.'

But she didn't look happy to Wingate. Although
she smiled and always answered his questions

cheerfully, there were shadows under her eyes. She never seemed to laugh like she had when she was at home. He was sure there was something wrong with her marriage but he didn't dare try to interfere between a husband and wife. Perhaps she wouldn't want him to interfere, especially as she always said everything was all right and never confided in him otherwise.

'What are you in town for?'

'We wanted supplies and Roy decided to combine that with some business meetings. I'm going to buy a new dress and some other bits and pieces.'

'Shall I meet you later and we'll have a coffee and something to eat?'

'I'd like that. We're not leaving until later on.'

'Good.' Wingate accompanied her to the door. As he opened it, the stagecoach thundered down the middle of the road. It came to a halt in a shower of mud by the livery stables where the horses were changed.

The guard got down, opened the door and helped out a woman, who Wingate recognised as the barber's wife. She was followed by a tall, lean man. Wingate didn't recognise him. He watched as the man spoke to the guard and then trudged off to the nearby boarding house. Trouble was the man didn't look like a cowboy seeking work.

'What's wrong?'

'Has Roy said anything about hiring more men?' Not that the stranger looked like a gunhand either.

'No. He doesn't discuss business with me, you know that. Why?'

'Nothing, honestly. You go along and do your shopping. I'll see you later.'

* * *

At the boarding house, McConnell asked for and was given a room overlooking the street. That way he could watch what was happening outside. The room wasn't large or elaborately furnished, but it was reasonably clean, he didn't have to share it with anyone and it was cheap and out of the way. Cheap, because, although $500 was a lot of money, it wouldn't last forever; and out of the way because he didn't want to attract attention to himself.

On the stagecoach here, he had remembered that, when they were riding together, Vaughan had said more than once how he wanted to be a rancher, with thousands of head of cattle and hundreds of horses. So he'd decided to look for him first amongst the ranching community, for which he'd need a map to find his way around, preferably one marked with the names of ranchers, or at least the ranches. As an excuse for wanting one, he thought he'd pretend to be on the look out for some homesteading land.

He also had to buy a horse and equipment.

First off though he had to wash and shave, change his shirt and get something to eat.

EIGHT

Reluctantly Vernon got up. He blinked at his reflection in the looking glass. Julie was right. He had to smarten himself up or he wouldn't be taken seriously, and if there was anything that was important to Vernon it was having others take him seriously. All the people he was seeing today – from the parson to his fellow ranchers – were important to impress if he was going to achieve their help in becoming Mayor. He'd set his heart on being appointed Mayor some while ago and wanted nothing to stand in his way, especially as it could lead to other, better and wealthier appointments. A position in the government of the area was surely not beyond someone of his capabilities.

After washing and dressing, he hurried out of the hotel. The smile and nods he gave to those he passed, hid a spurt of anger. Lane was meant to arrange for either Franklin or Poynton to act as his bodyguard while in town. Where the hell were they? He could be gunned down on the street while presumably they were sleeping off the excesses of the night before. He'd have to do something about Lane and soon. The man was getting above himself.

Thinking the only danger he was in was that of

being late, he hurried past the boarding house and turned down the sidestreet at the end of which was the church. At the same time McConnell left the boarding house, heading for town.

They missed one another by seconds.

Julie looked at her watch and gave an exclamation.

'What's the matter?' the seamstress asked.

'Oh nothing. I'm meant to be meeting my brother and I've delayed much too long.' Able to afford only one new dress, Julie had made the most out of trying them all on.

'Have you made up your mind which one you want, Mrs Vernon?'

'Yes, the green, no the red! The red one please.'

'I'll have it wrapped for you and sent over to the hotel. And the black shoes and gloves? They all go so well together.'

'Indeed they do.' Hastily Julie put on her jacket and the hat with the jaunty feather in it. Picking up her bag she dashed out of the dressmaker's.

Only to collide with Andrew McConnell, who was coming quickly along the sidewalk.

With a little cry, Julie was knocked off her feet.

McConnell had a view of white laced petticoats, frilly pantaloons and black stockings, making him grin in appreciation. He reached out to help her up. 'I'm sorry. Are you all right?'

Julie's hat had been knocked over one eye and her dignity, if not her body, was hurt by the encounter. 'You really should take more care!'

'Excuse me ma'am, but you were the one who came charging out and banged into me.'

'Why did you say you were sorry then?'

'I don't know. Here.' McConnell straightened

her hat. 'That's better.'

And suddenly the furious and embarrassed look left Julie's face and she giggled.

McConnell laughed back. 'You ain't hurt are you?'

'No, merely my pride. And it was my fault. I should be the one to say sorry. I've got to go. Goodbye.'

McConnell watched as the girl ran off down the sidewalk. He followed her and saw that she turned into the cafe, to which he too was headed. Inside, she had sat down next to a slightly older man, who had a marshal's star pinned to his vest. They were obviously brother and sister. Both had light brown eyes and fair, wavy hair, their heads bent towards one another, as they carried on their conversation.

McConnell watched them, without appearing to do so, a trick he'd picked up in prison when it was advantageous to know what the guards were up to. He was a bit dismayed to see that the lawman kept glancing his way. Trouble with the town marshal was the last thing he needed.

'So where the hell have you been?' Vernon demanded as he came out of the meeting with his fellow ranchers.

Tony Lane glowered down at his feet. Although he hated to admit it, he knew he was at fault. 'I'm sorry sir, we all overslept ...'

'Overslept! I don't pay you to goddamn oversleep!' Vernon broke off to smile and shake hands with another rancher.

'Good meeting Roy, we'll have that line through here any day now.'

It had been a good meeting, which was lucky for

Lane. In a good mood, Vernon was prepared to let his foreman get away with his lapse, this time. 'All right Tony, don't snivel,' he said nastily. 'It doesn't suit you. Now go and get the others. I'm ready to leave. I want to be home before it gets dark. Do you know where my wife is?'

'At the cafe.'

'With that blasted brother of hers I suppose? Fetch her then, and be quick. I'll meet you at the hotel.'

Lane left his boss. He couldn't tell whether he was glad he'd got away without suffering a tongue lashing or whether he'd have welcomed a bust-up.

Accompanied by Franklin and Poynton, who, despite their talk of bravado had been unwilling to face their angry boss, and had waited for him on the corner, Lane went into the cafe. Seeing Julie Vernon and her brother, he went up to the table. Ignoring Wingate, he said, 'Hallo, Mrs Vernon. Mr Vernon wants you. He's ready to leave.'

'I'll have to go,' Julie said, putting down her cup of coffee, not missing the look of annoyance that crossed Bart's face. He didn't like the way she always hastened to do whatever Roy said. Julie didn't like it either but it was a small price to pay if it kept Roy in a good temper. 'I'll see you later, Bart.'

As she got up, Lane put out a hand to take her arm. It was a gesture of help but Julie didn't miss the smirk on his face or the deliberate and unnecessary squeeze he gave her.

'Let's go, Mrs Vernon.'

And with Wingate trailing behind, Julie left the cafe in the company of the three men.

Outside she kissed Bart on the cheek and went

off with the others. Wingate watched for a moment before walking off in the other direction. It was a good thing Lane, Franklin and Poynton had been so pre-occupied with Julie that none of them had noticed McConnell sitting in the corner. As a stranger to Medicine Creek, he might have been shot down there and then; Franklin anyway reckless enough to do so in the hopeful knowledge that Vernon would protect him.

McConnell hadn't heard what was said between the girl and the man. But he'd been aware of undercurrents between them all. Oh well, it was nothing to do with him, he'd probably never see them again. But she had been pretty ...

He finished his meal and paying for it also left, heading for the real estate office. This was almost next door to the hotel, where Vernon and his men were getting ready to leave. Before the two men spotted one another, McConnell came to the real estate office and went inside. By the time he'd finished his business, the Vernons had left.

'Yes sir, how can I help you?' a rolypoly clerk asked.

'Have you got a map of the area? I'm interested in buying a piece of land to farm.'

The clerk looked down his nose a bit, probably preferring to deal with rich ranchers than poor sodbusters. Without a word, he pulled a rolled-up sheet of paper out from under the counter and smoothed it out.

McConnell peered at it. The map was marked neatly out into parcels of land. Unfortunately it listed no names of ranches or their owners. But when the clerk asked if it was satisfactory, he said it was because he could think of no way of asking for that information without arousing suspicion.

He took the map back to his room to study and work out the best route to take so that he could look over the ranches without wasting time. Unfortunately, there seemed to be a helluva lot of ground to cover.

While McConnell didn't want to do anything to single himself out, it soon became clear that the Marshal had indeed taken notice of him, just as McConnell feared.

The following morning when he was down at the livery stable picking out a horse to buy, the Marshal strolled ever so casually out to the corral and stopped by him, asking him his name.

'McConnell,' Andrew replied a bit sulkily. It wasn't fair. He felt sure lots of strangers came to town but he just bet that the Marshal didn't make a point of seeking them all out.

'Are you here looking for work?' Wingate went on.

'No.'

'Then may I ask your business here?'

'I'm a homesteader. Any objections?'

'You don't much look like a farmer.'

'What does a farmer look like? Look, Marshal, what are all these questions about? I ain't done anything.'

'Just make sure you keep it like that. This is a nice quiet town and believe me I intend to ensure it stays that way.'

Wingate walked off and McConnell watched him go, sure that the man didn't believe him. And equally sure that if he did anything out of line, then Wingate was going to be right there keeping an eye on him. But one thing about looking for Ray amongst the ranchers meant that Andrew didn't have to spend much time in the town itself.

NINE

The rolling country round Medicine Creek seemed never ending: the hills interspersed with grassy valleys, stands of cottonwoods beside small water-holes, grazing cattle. McConnell, who thought that during the last few days he must have covered every inch of it, was getting heartily tired of it and of searching unsuccessfully for Ray Vaughan. So unsuccessfully he was starting to think that maybe Joey Pemberton had been wrong and the letter to his brother hadn't come from Medicine Creek after all.

Or maybe he was wrong about Vaughan having become a rancher. Perhaps he'd discovered that such a life was too difficult, too full of chance, and had put the stolen money into something more secure. McConnell had kept a look out but he hadn't seen anyone vaguely resembling Ray around town either.

He had no idea of what he would do if he didn't find Ray, and soon. He couldn't pretend to be a homesteader for much longer without having the Marshal come after him, nor would the rest of his $500 last forever. He didn't much like the idea of doing nothing, except waiting to see if Ray sent someone else after him. But he couldn't stay in

Medicine Creek for ever searching for someone who might not be there. Where else to look? He didn't know.

It was hot, the air heavy and full of the scent of mountain flowers and McConnell was fed up. Swaying in time to his plodding horse, he fell asleep in the saddle. And woke up abruptly when the horse stumbled at the edge of a deep arroyo and, squealing, began to slide down the slope!

'Jesus Christ!' McConnell yelled out loud as he found himself tumbling off the back of the animal. He hit the side of the arroyo, made a frantic grab to hold on, and then, followed by his horse, slipped and slid towards the bottom.

As he did so, he saw a horse and rider below him, the horse's head bent to drink from the narrow stream of water still flowing along the centre of the wash.

Yelling, he landed with a painful thump, just about dodging his horse's hooves, as the animal landed nearby.

He heard the other horse whinney in fright, followed by a girl's scream, and a splash. Lying there dazed and bruised, he glanced over. The frightened horse was galloping away, while near him, sitting in the water, was the same young woman he'd bumped into in town. She was wearing riding skirt and boots so unfortunately he didn't get another satisfactory glimpse of drawers or legs. What he did get was a look at a furious face, because this time the accident had been all his fault.

'You again! You stupid idiot! What on earth did you think you were doing?' The girl scrambled to her feet. 'Look at me! I'm wet through, my horse has gone. Oooh you idiot!'

'Shut up lady,' McConnell muttered. He slowly sat up. His shoulder hurt but not too much. All the same he winced dramatically just to show her how badly he could have been hurt.

And as if realising she was making a great to-do about very little, she stopped her tirade and came over to him. 'What happened?'

'My horse fell down the arroyo. I fell off my horse. Thank you for your concern.'

'There's no need to be sarcastic.'

'There's no need for you to make such a fuss over a wet bottom, when I could have numerous broken bones.'

'You haven't have you?'

'No. But I could have.'

Julie ignored this. 'You gave me such a fright! Falling down practically on top of me like that. Are you sure you're all right?'

'Yeah, I think so.'

'I'm sorry for shouting at you.'

'No, you were right. I wasn't looking where I was going. It should be me apologising this time.'

'Can you walk?'

McConnell tried doing so. Like his horse, which was standing nearby, he was trembling but nothing sent bolts of pain through him, so he decided that was just reaction and nothing worse. He limped over to the animal, patting it reassuringly. Of the girl's horse there was no sign. He turned back to where she stood watching him anxiously.

'How far away do you live?'

'Beyond the next ridge of hills.'

'I'd better take you home.'

'Oh no. It's all right.'

'No, it ain't. You're wet, you've had a fright and

I'm responsible. I insist.'

Julie looked doubtful, scared almost.

'Come on, you ain't frightened of me are you? I know I keep bashing into you and knocking you over but I'm really perfectly harmless.'

She smiled. It was a nice smile that lit up her whole face. 'Yes, I believe you are.'

'The name's Andrew McConnell by the way.'

'Julie Vernon.'

They shook hands and saying, 'Let's go then.' McConnell mounted, helping her up behind him. She put her arms round his waist and he spurred the horse up the other side of the arroyo. In front of him fifty or so cows grazed in a lush meadow bordered by round topped hills, covered with swaying trees. 'This is good land.'

'What are you doing way out here?'

'Looking for homestead land to farm,' McConnell kept up the lie.

'Well you won't find it here. All this belongs to my husband.'

Damn! She was married. And McConnell realised that he'd been starting to enjoy impossible dreams about her. A young lady like this wouldn't have anything to do with him, even if she could, which she couldn't.

'You know that homesteaders aren't always welcome by ranchers don't you?'

'There seems to be enough for everyone. I ain't heard of any trouble like that round here.'

'That's because there aren't many homesteaders.'

'What do you think?'

'If my opinion mattered, I'd say the same as you. There's plenty of land.'

'Of course your opinion matters.'

'Does it?'

McConnell was surprised at the bitterness in her voice. Something was making her sad. He wanted to ask her what it was, even though it was none of his business and he had enough troubles of his own. Fearing a rebuff, he kept quiet.

As they got closer to the foothills, Julie became quiet. It was almost as if she didn't want to go home. Or at least not with him. And as soon as the ranch buildings came into sight, she said,

'You'd better let me down here. I can walk the rest of the way.'

'Don't be silly.'

'You don't understand. My husband is wary of strangers and he gets jealous easily.'

'He has no need.'

'I know that, so do you, he doesn't. Please.'

But before either of them could say any more, or do anything, riders appeared from the direction of the barn. As they got closer, McConnell felt Julie stiffen against him. When the riders pulled up by them, he recognised the men as those who had come into the cafe and collected her. The leader was big and beefy with the large reddened nose of a habitual drinker – surely he wasn't her husband!

'What's going on here? Who the hell are you? Mrs Vernon are you OK?'

'Of course I am, Tony. I fell off my horse in the arroyo.'

'You shouldn't have been out on your own.'

McConnell glared at Lane, not liking the tone he used.

'You know Mr Vernon don't like it. Let's go see him, shall we? You too.'

'I'll leave her with you now,' McConnell said, not

liking the situation and not wanting to get involved.

'No you won't asshole. You ain't going anywhere except with us.'

'There's no need to be rude,' Julie protested. 'He was only helping me.'

The only reason McConnell didn't make a fuss was that the girl was still riding behind him and liable to be hurt. Otherwise he'd have told Lane exactly what to do with his orders.

As they rode up towards the house, the three cowboys flanking McConnell, the door opened and a man stepped out onto the verandah.

Several things happened at once!

'Ray! Oh my God!' This time, the girl behind him or not, there was no way McConnell couldn't react. He shoved her off the horse and surrounded as he was by Vaughan's men, who had already shown themselves hostile to him, went for his gun, as much for his own protection as to shoot anyone, especially as the other man was already yelling:

'It's him! McConnell! Get him you fools!'

Lane knew he wasn't a good enough gunman to beat someone already drawing his gun; probably Franklin and Poynton weren't either. So he launched himself at McConnell.

The two men went down in the dust before the house. Immediately Franklin and Poynton leapt from their horses and rushed over, kicking and hitting where they could.

Horrified, Julie rushed up on the porch, grabbing at Vernon's arm. 'Stop them! Stop them, please!'

'Be quiet!' And pushing her to one side, Vernon went up to the rail, leaning against it, watching, a grin of anticipation on his face.

McConnell was taking quite a beating. Against Lane, who was a slugger with no finesse, he might have stood some sort of chance. Against three of them he didn't have any.

He was dragged to his feet, punched several times and knocked down again. On the ground he was kicked in ribs, back and buttocks. Hands then pulled him up again, held him while he was thumped in the stomach. Let go, he fell again.

Andrew could hear them laughing, yelling, panting with exertion and pleasure. Blood in his eyes, he could no longer see them. He thought he heard Julie crying out. All he could do was try to protect himself and he feared he was about to be beaten to death.

'All right that's enough!' Vernon yelled. 'Stop it!' He strode off the porch and catching hold of Lane's shoulder, pulled him backwards almost off his feet, shoving him away.

For a moment, Lane looked at him mad-eyed, breathing heavily, fists clenched as if he wanted to attack his employer. Then the madness died out of his eyes and he calmed down. Following his lead the other two did the same. And all of them stared down at McConnell, lying in their midst, bloody, bruised, clothes torn and dusty.

'Get up,' Vernon ordered.

Easier said than done, McConnell thought. He got to one knee, putting a hand to his cut lips. Jesus but he hurt!

Impatiently, Vernon reached forward jerking him up. McConnell swayed on his feet but managed to stay upright, more or less.

'Lane, you and the others can go now.'

'Are you sure?'

'Yes. I can handle Mr McConnell.'

Once the three men walked away, Julie ran down from the porch. She caught hold of Andrew's arm. 'How could you let that happen?' she accused her husband.

'Shut up Julie you don't know what you're talking about. Go to the house and don't interfere.'

'No, Roy, I'm going to see to his bruises.'

Vernon stared at her in amazement. It was the first time in a long while that she'd bothered to defy him. His hand itched to hit her. But not out here in the open. That pleasure would come later. As Julie went by him, he caught her arm. 'First of all before you become a ministering angel, I want to know what happened. Why were you riding behind him? How come your skirt is all wet?'

'It's nothing to worry about Roy. I had an accident on my horse that's all.'

'And McConnell just happened to be riding by?'

'Yes.'

'I don't believe you.'

'I really don't care.'

For a moment husband and wife looked at one another. It was Vernon who broke the gaze, flinging her arm from him.

'Oh, for God's sake get him into the house and get him patched up. And be quick about it. We need to have a talk. Sort things out. And, darling, I really don't need your help with that!'

Ignoring him, Julie said, 'Come along, Mr McConnell.' And she helped Andrew into the house. She looked back at Roy. He'd sat down in a rocking chair, staring moodily down at the cowboys who had gathered round Lane, asking excited questions. She had the awful feeling that he'd only stopped the beating because so many witnesses had gathered.

TEN

'Oh dear, Mr McConnell, I'm so sorry for what happened.' Carefully Julie bathed the cut over Andrew's left eye.

'It wasn't your fault. Ouch!'

'I'm sorry.'

McConnell suddenly grinned. 'We seem to spend all our time apologising to one another.'

Julie smiled hesitantly back. 'You'd better take off your shirt.'

McConnell did so. The knife wound down his arm had started to bleed again.

'That looks bad. Perhaps you ought to see the doctor in town about it. How did it happen?'

'It was an accident.' McConnell didn't elaborate.

'How do you feel?'

'Like I've been run over by a herd of cattle. But I'll be OK.' He'd survived worse in prison, although he didn't tell her that. And he had to admit that being looked after by a concerned young woman, with tears in her eyes and gentle hands, was far better than any of the treatment he'd received in the prison hospital. It was also quite nice the way her body moved near to his. He told himself to stop thinking that way. She was a married woman; the wife of his enemy. And her brother was the suspicious marshal. Hell!

'There, that looks a bit better anyway but you're going to be a fine sight when all those bruises come out.'

'Mrs Vernon, who were those men who did this to me?'

'Tony Lane is my husband's foreman, and the two hands were Franklin and Poynton. I neither like nor approve of any of them.'

'They don't look much like cowhands to me.'

'Lane is experienced with cattle. The other two aren't. They haven't been here very long. You're not going to do anything silly about them are you?'

'One against three, hardly. Anyway I daresay they were only following your husband's orders.' Before Julie could ask what he meant, he went on, 'I'd better go out to Ray. Let's see what sort of cockeyed story he's about to tell me.'

'Ray? My husband's name is Roy.'

Painfully McConnell got to his feet. 'It was Ray when I knew him.'

As he got to the door, Julie said. 'Be careful.'

McConnell nodded and went out, leaving her puzzled and unhappy.

On the porch, Vaughan, or Vernon as he evidently was now, had poured out drinks: excellent whisky in cut-glass tumblers. All very civilised, McConnell thought with a sneer. Unlike prison tin cups filled with warm, stale water.

'Sit down, Andy. I'm sorry about all that.'

'Sure you are.'

'No, really I am. I shouldn't have let it go on as long as it did. But you went for your gun and I thought you'd come here to kill me.'

'If I was going to do that I'd hardly have had

your wife riding behind me.'

'I wasn't to know what sort of person ten years in prison had turned you into.'

'Not the sort to hide behind a woman. And I wouldn't have spent ten years in prison if it hadn't been for you.'

Vernon ignored that, saying instead, 'By the way, where did you meet her?'

'Like she said she had an accident and fell off her horse. Down by the arroyo. That's all.' McConnell remembered what Julie had told him about her husband. 'Not jealous are you Ray?'

'Roy, please.'

'There's no need to be. None of it was her fault either.'

McConnell picked up the glass and drank some of the whisky. It was strange to be sitting here on the porch, Ray Vaughan, the man who for ten years he'd considered a traitor and had wanted to kill, across from him, the pair of them drinking whisky together. What he felt he probably ought to be doing was telling him to go for his gun. The question was how far could he be trusted now.

'You know, Andy, I never meant to do what I did. I acted on the spur of the moment. I was always ashamed of it afterwards.'

'Oh yeah? So ashamed you let me rot in jail for ten years.'

'It wouldn't have done either of us any good if I'd given myself up, would it?'

'All the time I was waiting for my trial I believed there was some mistake. That someone else had hit me and forced you to go away, leaving me to face the law on my own. I thought you'd come and break me out.' McConnell laughed. 'You really must have thought me stupid.'

'Oh no it wasn't like that! We were friends.'

'Friends, goddammit Ray!'

'Roy. Please try to remember.' Vernon shook his head sadly. 'I don't know what came over me. It was just the thought of all that money. I didn't realize we would get so much from the robbery and it meant that I could do what I'd always wanted and start up my own ranch. I could be successful.'

'You've certainly been that,' McConnell said bitterly. He stared down at the land spreading out all round the house. Some way down the slope of the hill on which the house was built were the ranch's work buildings – bunkhouse, barns, blacksmith's, all neat and tidy. Prime horseflesh grazed in large corrals, and beyond them again were the meadows full of cattle, fattening up for market.

'You might have got your dream but didn't you ever think I had dreams of my own? All I got was ten years in prison. You ever been in prison Ray, Roy?'

'No.'

'It ain't easy believe me. I wouldn't wish it on my worst enemy, let alone my best friend! And then when I do get out what do I find but Black Jack Pemberton waiting to stick a knife into me.'

'What else could I do? You threatened me at your trial, swore vengeance. You had every right to be mad at me …'

'Mad! I could have torn you to bits.'

'There, you see. And for all I knew you still felt the same way. You might have been coming after me. I'll admit it, Andy, I've built up a good life here. I've got my ranch, a beautiful home, a lovely wife. And I'm an important person in town. I'm on the Town Council, my fellow ranchers seek out and respect my opinion. I don't want to lose it all.'

McConnell made an angry noise in his throat and stared down at the ground, clenching his fists.

'I wanted you out of my way ...'

'Killed, is the word.'

'Yes, all right then, killed. I hired Black Jack ... what happened to him anyway?'

'He got unlucky.'

'Oh. I thought he must have done. Which is why I told my men to watch for you and to shoot you on sight. Now I know I was wrong.'

'You do?'

'Yes.'

'And what exactly has brought about this sudden change of heart?'

'We were once good pals weren't we? OK perhaps too much has happened for us to be good pals again. Even so, I want to let bygones be bygones. Don't you?' Vernon looked McConnell straight in the eye like he used to and smiled slightly.

'You owe me,' McConnell said, making a feeble attempt to gain the upper hand, determined not to let Vernon off that lightly. But he could feel the situation slipping from his grasp, just like his arguments always had when faced with the other man's silvery tongue.

'Sure I do, Andy. I know that. And I'm going to make it up to you if I can.'

'How? Ten years is a long time.'

'I'll pay you.'

'You believe that money can make up for what happened?'

'Not really, no. What else can I offer you? I'm not about to give you a share of my ranch and surely you don't expect me to go into town and say to Bart Wingate 'Hey remember that bank robbery ten years ago, I was the other guy involved'? Be reasonable Andy.'

'Reasonable!'

'Yes, reasonable. Why not? There would be a condition though.'

'What exactly?'

'Don't look so suspicious. It's not much. I want you to leave Medicine Creek. This isn't your home so that shouldn't be too difficult. But it is *my* home. Like I said I'm well respected here. I'm going to run for Mayor. I don't want anything or anyone to foul that up. You stay around I'd always be scared you'd get drunk and start spouting the truth or else someone might start asking questions as to where you got your money from. But if I have your word that you'll go away and never come back then there's no problem. But if you decide you'd rather have revenge than money then I shall do all in my power to stop you. I don't want it to come to that but if it does, I'll win. And you'll end up with nothing. This way at least you get something.'

McConnell sat back in the chair. Running a hand through his hair, he thought things over. Damn Vaughan, or Vernon, whatever his goddamned name was! And damn the thugs he employed. He ought to throw Vernon's offer back in his face. Money couldn't make up for the misery of jail. But short of killing Vernon, McConnell could see no other way of getting revenge; no one was likely to listen to him if he called the man a bank-robber any more now than they had before. And it would be difficult to kill him, when he was surrounded by the likes of Tony Lane. Besides Andrew knew that when push came to shove he wouldn't be able to kill someone in cold blood.

And reluctant commonsense told him that in any fight with Vernon he'd come off worse, one way or the other.

Money might not be a completely satisfactory answer, but at least it would help him make a fresh start.

'How much?'

'How about the original amount we stole plus ten per cent for each of those ten years.'

'You've got that much?'

Vernon laughed. 'Look around, Andy. I'm a rich man! What do you say? You don't really want to kill me do you? I certainly don't want to kill you.'

'All right,' McConnell agreed, seeing no other choice.

'Good.' Vernon smiled broadly. He rubbed his hands together. 'It's for the best. No use harbouring old grudges. I'll come into town tomorrow and make arrangements to get the money out of the bank. Where are you staying?'

McConnell told him.

'I'm glad it's all turned out like this. I know you can never fully forgive me for what I did, God I can't forgive myself, but at least this way I can know I've done my best by you. Ah here comes Julie.'

'Dinner's ready. Mr McConnell would you like to stay to eat?'

'Of course he would.' Vernon stood up clapping an arm round McConnell's shoulders. 'Let's go inside. Don't look so worried my dear. Everything is all right between us now. Isn't that so, Andy?'

'Yeah.'

ELEVEN

It was very late by the time McConnell reached Medicine Creek and he hurt all over. His whole body felt like it was bruised, ribs aching so much he could hardly sit in the saddle, having to lean forward over the pommel, groaning with every painful jar of his body.

He hadn't much liked dinner with the two Vernons. He felt ill-at-ease in Roy's presence, and Julie hardly spoke. The only one seeming not to feel any discomfort in the situation was Vernon himself. He always had been able to talk the hindleg off a donkey, and he talked endlessly about how he'd found this ranch, thought it perfect and settled down. And how happy he was now that he was married and hoped to have children. At which he smiled broadly at Julie. McConnell glanced at Julie too. She didn't appear to share her husband's sentiments. There was something clearly wrong between them and McConnell was only too happy when it was time to leave.

Stabling his horse, he walked through the deserted streets to the boarding house and wearily climbed the stairs to his room. Once there, he pulled off his boots, decided he was too tired to bother to undress any further and collapsed on the bed. Sometime in the night he woke up and got under the blanket but that was all he remembered.

'Wake up asshole!'

The voice was harsh and loud. McConnell blinked open his eyes and saw Marshal Wingate standing over him, gun drawn and pointed unwaveringly at his forehead. For a moment Andrew was taken back to the other time he'd woken up to be faced by a Sheriff and a posse. But he hadn't committed a bank robbery this time, hadn't done anything wrong.

'On your stomach!' Wingate ordered and prodded him in the side with the gun.

Dazed and puzzled, McConnell rolled over. His face was pushed into the pillow, a knee pressed in the small of his back and he was quickly handcuffed.

'What's going on?'

'You're under arrest for robbery.'

'Robbery! Jesus Christ, Marshal!' McConnell tried to sit up but he was pushed back down.

'Stay where you are.'

'I ain't done anything.'

'Oh no?' Wingate began to move around the room, opening drawers, peering at McConnell's clothes. 'Where is it?'

'Where's what?'

'The money you took from Mr Simms' store last night.'

'I don't know what the hell you're talking about.' Taking a risk on being shot, McConnell squirmed over on his back and sat up.

Wingate paused from searching through McConnell's things to look over at him. 'Late last night someone broke into Mr Simms' store. Mr Simms came down from his bedroom and the thief knocked him out. Whoever it was stole twenty dollars from the cash register.'

'Someone, you said. So why come here?'

'Mr Simms got a good enough look at his assailant to describe him.'

'He's lying.'

'Why would he do that?'

'Or mistaken.'

'I don't think so.'

'God, Marshal, I didn't do it.'

'You were out all day yesterday.'

'Yeah and when I got back I came here and went to bed. Look at me.' McConnell wondered if he looked as bad as he felt. 'Could I go out robbing stores with all these bruises?'

'Perhaps that happened to you afterwards.'

'Well it didn't.'

'So you admit the robbery?'

'No, of course I don't. Don't try to trick me. I mean it didn't happen afterwards or before because I didn't do it.' But McConnell's heart was sinking fast. The Marshal didn't believe him. No one else would believe him. It was the word of a stranger against that of a citizen.

Wingate believed him even less when he found a couple of hundred dollars in McConnell's bag. 'Where did you get this?'

This was going from bad to worse. If McConnell told him about Black Jack Pemberton he'd have to tell him about being in jail for bank robbery. Not quick-witted enough to think up any plausible story, he sat gaping at Wingate in something like horror.

'Looks like you make a good living out of robbery.'

'No! It's legitimate money! You've gotta believe me.'

'Give me one good reason why I should.'

'I'm innocent. If I had all that money why would I steal twenty dollars?'

'Come on. Twenty dollars here, twenty dollars there, that's how you've got this much.'

'If I'd robbed Mr Simms' store would I be foolish enough to come back here and go to sleep with the proceeds of the robbery not even hidden?'

'I've known a lot of outlaws who've done a lot more foolish things than that. If they weren't foolish they wouldn't be outlaws in the first place. I don't want your sort round here, neither will the judge.' Wingate's eyes and voice hardened. 'It's goddamned lucky for you that Mr Simms isn't too badly hurt. He's respected in this town and it might have been that if you'd hit him harder and a lynch-mob had formed, I wouldn't have done all that much to stop it. Now come on you little bastard, get the hell up!'

Scared that Wingate was going to lose his temper and forget he was a lawman, McConnell slowly eased himself off the bed, his whole body crying out in protest. 'Can I at least put my boots on?'

'OK, but carefully.' Taking no chances, Wingate moved McConnell's gun and rifle from the chair by the bed, putting them on the far side of the room. 'Remember I'd like nothing more'n to be given the excuse to shoot you.'

'Don't worry, I ain't about to get shot over a mistake.'

'It's no mistake.'

Wingate unlocked the handcuffs and with the gun pointed steadily at him, McConnell pulled on his boots. He groaned now and then but got no sign of sympathy. After he'd shrugged into his vest, Wingate indicated for him to put his hands behind his back and he was again handcuffed.

Wingate picked up the guns and the money. 'Let's go.'

'What about my things?'

'I'll send my deputy for them. Not that you'll need 'em where you're going.'

Feeling numb, McConnell led the way down the stairs and out into the street, aware of the Marshal and his gun close behind him. Everyone who was about, and it seemed like it was the whole damn town, turned to watch as he was marched towards the jail. Quite a crowd had gathered in front of the store, peering in the window, speaking animatedly to one another. As Wingate and McConnell came into view, they all went quiet and looked over at them. McConnell began to shake with fear. Supposing they made a dash for him? Dragged him down, tried to kill him? It was as bad as last time. Worse. Now he wasn't guilty.

He'd been set-up again. Roy Vernon had set him up. And he'd believed the sonofabitch! Believed his lying words and his false smile. Believed that Roy would be willing to buy him off. Looked forward to having a lot of money. And here he was being put in jail to face another prison sentence. For robbery with violence. Christ, he'd get more than ten years for that, especially if they found out he'd only been out of jail for a few weeks. Eyes misting with tears, he stumbled.

Wingate caught his arm. 'Get on!'

The jailhouse door slammed shut behind them. Wingate shoved him through to the cells and pushed him into one. Undoing the handcuffs he locked the door.

It wasn't long before he was back. This time he had with him a pale looking little man, with a bandage round his head. Mr Simms.

The man peered hesitantly into the cells and Wingate spoke to him gently. 'Now, Mr Simms, take your time. He's behind bars and can't hurt you. You, McConnell, get on up and come forward. Take a good look at him Mr Simms, and then tell me if he's the man who broke into your store last night and attacked you.'

'Tell him you were wrong about me,' McConnell pleaded. 'Tell him I wasn't the one. Please.'

Simms turned to Wingate. 'It's him all right. I'd recognise him anywhere.'

'You lying bastard!' McConnell screamed and grabbed at the bars.

Simms cried out in startled fear.

'Get back!' Wingate yelled at McConnell, clanging at the bars with his gun.

'He's lying!' McConnell shouted as Wingate ushered Simms out.

'Shut up! Come along Mr Simms, don't worry.'

'Oh God,' Andrew moaned as he was left alone. He sank back on the bunk. He put his head in his hands, desperate. He couldn't go to jail again. He couldn't.

'Well that's that then,' Wingate said later on. 'You've been positively identified. So all you've gotta do is wait for your trial. Judge should be here in a few weeks' time.'

'You're so very sure I done it ain't you?'

'I figured you for trouble the first moment I saw you. All that damn nonsense about looking for homestead land! You don't look like a farmer, you look like jailbait. Now, I'd advise you to keep quiet and not do anything to upset me. Or you might get another beating to go with the one you've already had. By the way, who was responsible for all those bruises?'

'Your bastard brother-in-law.'

TWELVE

'Well I don't know why old man Vernon didn't let us kill the sonofabitch when we had the chance.' Sulkily Dennis Franklin fingered the butt of one of his guns, as if longing to draw and fire it at any target that presented itself. 'We could easily have followed him back to town and put several bullets in his body.'

He, Lane and Poynton stood at a corner of the corral, watching a wrangler break horses. It was tough, bone-breaking work and Franklin thought the man doing it was a fool – risking his limbs, perhaps even his life, all for fifty dollars a month. He'd never do anything stupid like that.

Lane made sure no one was listening. 'The boss thought there were too many people who knew McConnell had been here and that we'd had a fight. To find his body on the trail to town would have been too much of a coincidence. He thought it better to accuse McConnell of robbery and get him sent back to jail.'

'Me and Mal are going to move on lessen there's some excitement around here. Ain't that right, Mal?'

'Yeah.' Poynton was quite ready to go.

'Will you come with us Tony?'

'Mebbe. It all depends.'

'What on?'

Julie Vernon, Lane thought, but said vaguely, 'Oh this and that. But I shouldn't worry too much. I reckon you might still get your chance to kill McConnell.'

'How come?'

'Vernon believes that McConnell won't say anything about his past, on account of the fact that he's been in jail before and that would look bad for him. Mebbe even double his sentence. If you were McConnell, what would you do?'

Franklin thought hard for a moment. His thought processes not being all that quick, he had to admit he didn't know.

'Well iffen I was him, either at the trial, or even before, I'd tell everyone I could about whatever it was happened in the past. If McConnell does the same, it won't make any difference to his situation, he'll still be found guilty. And everyone will say they don't believe him. But mud sticks. And nobody will vote someone in for Mayor, who just might have done something to be ashamed of. And you know how important becoming Mayor is to the boss.'

'I don't see what Vernon can do about it now,' Poynton said, wincing as the horse bucked the wrangler off and he landed with a wrenching jar. 'McConnell is in jail.'

'There are all sorts of ways he can be got at.'

Franklin grinned. 'Let's hope Vernon decides to do something.'

'I have a feeling he will. Even if McConnell keeps quiet, Vernon will be scared he won't. He's made a mistake and he'll want to put it right.'

* * *

Vernon was thinking much the same, especially when a couple of days later Bart Wingate came out to the ranch. Wingate rarely came to the Rocking V. It was a long way from town, which meant he had to spend the whole day away. He didn't like Vernon, a fact about which Roy was well aware. And even if there was any sort of trouble, such as rustlers, because he was town marshal it wasn't anything to do with Wingate, but was left to the county sheriff to deal with. Unless this was a social visit, which Vernon doubted, the only reason he was here could be to do with McConnell.

'Hi Bart,' Vernon said when the man dismounted in front of the house. He was prepared to lie and deceive; something he'd always been good at and, with long practice, was getting better at all the time. 'This is an unexpected pleasure. Julie will be pleased to see you. Or at least … it's not a law matter that's brought you way out here is it?'

'Sort of.' Wingate walked up the steps on to the verandah.

'Come on inside where it's cooler. Julie! Look who's here.'

Julie hurried into the hall from the kitchen where she'd been helping the cook with some baking. Brother and sister embraced.

Vernon smiled to hide his annoyance at their closeness. He was scared that one day that closeness would lead Julie to tell Bart the truth about her marriage. As far as Vernon was concerned, he felt he'd done nothing wrong. A wife's place was strictly a subordinate one and she should do what she was told. Julie had to learn that; once she had they would get on fine. He had an idea Wingate wouldn't see it in quite the same way.

Leading the way into the parlour, he poured out iced lemonade. 'Sit down.' He made sure he sat next to Julie, leaving Bart to sit across from them. He put a hand on Julie's. To others it would look like a gesture of affection. To Julie it was a warning. 'Now, Bart, what are you here for?'

'I've got a prisoner in my jail at the moment ...'

'A prisoner! You make it sound mighty important.'

'Let's say he ain't just a Saturday night drunk. He's accused of robbing and attacking old Mr Simms.'

'Good God! I hope Simms wasn't badly hurt.'

'Luckily, no.'

'I don't see why you've come here about him. What has he to do with me?'

'The man's name is Andrew McConnell and he says he was out here the day before his arrest when your men beat him up.'

At the mention of the name, Julie had given an involuntary gasp of 'Oh no', which Vernon stifled with a squeeze of her hand. Now she sat looking at her brother with dismay in her eyes.

'Is that true?'

Vernon let Julie go and sipped at his lemonade to gain time. 'Yes, in a way.'

'Mind telling me why it happened?'

'It was a mistake.'

'A mistake that left McConnell with cuts and bruises on his face and bruises all over his body. The beating must have lasted quite a while for him to have gotten so hurt.'

'Three of my men were involved, that's why it

was so bad. It was over as soon as I could stop it.'

'I see. And why did they beat McConnell up?'

'Like I said it was a mistake. Julie had been out riding. Her horse returned on its own and naturally we were all very worried. I was actually getting ready to ride out to find her. When McConnell rode up with Julie riding behind him, my men naturally feared the worst and set about him.'

Even Vernon thought it was a lame excuse but it was the best he'd been able to come up with. Before Wingate could find any flaws in it, he hurried on. 'You must understand it all happened so quickly. Of course when Julie told me McConnell had done nothing wrong, in fact had helped her, I stopped them. Isn't that right sweetheart?'

Julie reluctantly nodded.

'I was so sorry about it all, I allowed Julie to patch Mr McConnell up and then invited him to dinner. He seemed a nice enough young man, yet you say he's in jail for robbery?'

'That's right.'

'I'm sure he's not a thief,' Julie said.

'Doesn't seem much doubt. Old Mr Simms has identified him.'

'When is the trial?'

'When the circuit judge gets here. Couple of weeks time probably.'

'The sooner the better I say. People like that shouldn't be allowed to walk the streets. Congratulations Marshal on catching him so quickly.'

'It was easy. He didn't even try to run. I suppose he hoped Simms wouldn't be able to identify him.'

'Thieves do strange things.'

Once Wingate had gone, Julie couldn't contain

herself any longer. 'Why didn't you tell Bart the truth?'

'I did.'

'No you didn't. You and Mr McConnell recognised one another. That was what the fight was about. Not me.'

'You don't know what you're talking about.'

'And you didn't stop him being beaten up because of anything I said either.'

'You just be quiet Julie. It's about time you learned that I'm your husband and it's to me you owe your loyalty.' A familiar glint came into Vernon's eyes. He grabbed her arm, squeezing it painfully. 'Perhaps as you were so quick to defend McConnell, I was right when I suspected there was something going on between you and him.'

'Of course there isn't. Don't be silly.'

'What the hell happened between the two of you out there in the arroyo? You were alone together for God knows how long.'

'Oh Roy, nothing happened.' Tears came into the girl's eyes as she tried unsuccessfully to free herself from his grip.

'If I find you're cheating on me you get kicked out of here, you understand? Then you'll have no choice but to go back to Medicine Creek and live in the squalor from which I rescued you.'

'I didn't live in squalor.'

'Your parents were poor. You were poor. Your father was a clerk who worked in a general store. You lived in a three-room shack. Now look at what you've got. Glass in the windows, pine furniture imported from the East, servants. Surely my dear you don't want to give all this up and go back to living with your brother, do you? Think of all the gossip and the shame, because I shall make very sure everyone knows that I had no choice but to get rid of you because you've been whoring with a convicted thief.'

All this time Vernon had been squeezing Julie's arm. He wouldn't stop until she cried out or begged him. She tried hard not to give him the satisfaction of doing either. Finally she couldn't help herself. 'Please, Roy, stop, you're hurting me.'

With a savage grin he let her go, shoving her against the wall. 'Just forget about McConnell or telling anyone else that he's innocent. I mean it. Now sweetheart,' with one of his swift, unaccountable swings of mood, he took her arm, gently this time and kissed her cheek, 'let's go and see how the men are getting on breaking those new horses. Smile for me dear, that's right, there's nothing to worry about. I forgive you, this time.'

THIRTEEN

'Just had word, McConnell, Judge will be arriving in town in a couple of days time. Your trial can begin as soon as he's ready.'

'Oh good,' McConnell replied sarcastically. 'I can't wait.'

'I reckon the trial'll be the high point of the year. Everyone will want to attend. Medicine Creek will be packed to capacity.'

McConnell had been in jail over two weeks now. At first he insisted on protesting his innocence but had soon given up. The Marshal thought he was lying. The evidence was too great.

Even so, Wingate was surprised to discover that he quite liked his prisoner and one evening, when it was quiet and he was bored sitting in the office all by himself, he brought in a chequers board. 'Do you play?'

'Yeah, sometimes.'

So every evening the pair of them played chequers. McConnell lost nearly every time, Wingate being a clever and sly player who knew all the tricks going. They talked about this and that at the same time and Wingate had the feeling that McConnell wasn't telling him everything about his past.

Now, McConnell said, 'Who's the judge?'

'Herbert Neely. He's an oldtimer. Been riding the circuit up here last seven or eight years or so. Before that he was down in Colorado. Got too tame for him there.'

'Oh shit.' McConnell sat down on the bunk.

'What's up?'

'Nothing,' McConnell lied. Herbert Neely was the judge who'd presided at his trial. Was it possible that he'd remember the young Andrew McConnell from ten years ago?

'Still sharp as a tack,' Wingate went on and, confirming McConnell's worst fears, added, 'Says he can remember the names, if not the faces, of anyone he's ever sentenced. Don't see how that can be myself but then I ain't clever enough to be a judge. You sure you're OK? You look awful white.'

'I'm all right. Just feel a bit sick is all.' Sick at heart anyway, McConnell thought, and lay back on the bunk, staring up at the ceiling. 'Leave me alone for a while.'

'Mr McConnell, Andy.'

McConnell stopped his moody contemplation of the cell wall, rolled over on the bunk and blinked in surprise. 'Julie, er Mrs Vernon.'

As he got up, she smiled. 'Julie will be fine.'

'What are you doing here?'

'My husband and some of the men have come in to attend your trial. I demanded to come as well.' The few words hid the amount of begging Julie had had to do before Roy agreed to her accompanying him. Even then, it had been with the threat that he'd be keeping a careful eye on her. However, it wasn't that careful an eye, it had prevented him heading straight for the saloon. And quite what he thought she was going to get up to with Andrew when he was behind bars, she didn't know.

'Does he know you're here?'

She shook her head. 'Nor does Bart. Neither of them would approve. Roy doesn't trust me and Bart never did like me taking an interest, or interfering as he put it, in the law and what he did. He always said it was too dangerous.'

'What are you doing here then?'

'Because something is wrong.'

'It is. I didn't rob anyone.'

'Roy told Bart a very plausible story about why you were beaten up at the ranch. It wasn't true. I was there. I heard you yell out "Ray" when you saw him and Roy said something like "It's him, get him".'

'Have you asked Roy what it was all about?'

'Yes, he said I was mistaken.'

'Does Bart know?'

'No, not yet. You see I wasn't sure whether the beating up had anything to do with the robbery. Has it?'

'Yeah.'

'How?'

McConnell came closer, clutching at the bars. 'Your husband is a lying bastard, Julie, and a thief as well.'

'Oh.' She went red and put a hand to her mouth in shock, although why she should be so surprised she wasn't sure. She had known for a long time that Roy wasn't the paragon of virtue he presented to the outside world.

'I'm sorry if you don't believe me.' McConnell sounded disappointed.

'But I think I do. Please, tell me everything.'

And, faced with someone willing to listen to him, willing to believe him, Andrew did so. When he'd finished he could see tears in the girl's eyes and wondered who they were for: him, Roy or herself?

'You really didn't rob Mr Simms?'

'No.'

'And you think Roy somehow fixed it to look like you did?'

'I know that's what happened.'

'But how? Why would Mr Simms lie?'

'Perhaps he was bribed, or threatened.'

'You say Roy wanted to get you thrown into jail and out of harm's way, but surely it would have been easier just to kill you? This way you could tell Bart all about Roy being a bank-robber. If that sort of thing got round town it would destroy him.'

'Who would believe me against him?'

'Some people might. Andy, why haven't you told Bart?'

'Because Roy had me figured right. He knew I'd keep quiet. You see what happened then between Roy and me wouldn't make any difference to my being accused of robbery with violence, except to make me look guiltier than I do already in most people's eyes. And there's probably no connection between Roy and Mr Simms to show that the storeowner could have been forced into lying about me.'

'None that anyone knows about anyway,' Julie agreed. 'But won't what happened be discovered anyway?'

'I was hoping it wouldn't. We're a long way from Colorado, it happened over ten years ago. I don't think there was ever a Wanted poster out on me.

Not that that makes any difference now,' McConnell added in a mumble, thinking of Judge Neely.

'Why did you come here? Why didn't you go back home?'

'I couldn't. I'd already brought enough shame on my family by becoming a bank-robber. How could I bring more by going home and starting all the neighbours talking about the McConnells and their outlaw son?'

'You'd served your time. Any gossip would have died down after a while and I bet your parents would have forgiven you and welcomed you home.'

'Ma maybe, not Pa.'

Early on, his mother had undertaken the arduous journey to the prison to see him. The visits had stopped when his father found out about them. But she continued to write and in her letters she always begged him to go home on his release, saying that his father would forgive him once he saw him.

'Anyway it's too late now, ain't it?'

Julie's eyes filled with tears. She stepped closer to the bars and, to his surprise, put her hands over McConnell's. Slowly he turned his palms upwards and they gripped one another's hands tightly. It seemed to him as if he was destined to always be on the other side of bars to someone he ached to take into his arms.

'Is there anything I can do?'

'You believe in me, that's enough.'

The door to the cell block banged open, causing them both to jump guiltily and spring apart.

'Oh Julie, hallo,' Wingate said. 'What are you doing here?'

'I came to see Mr McConnell. He helped me the other day. I can't believe he's guilty.'

'This is no place for you.' With a harsh look at McConnell, as if in some way he'd encouraged her, Wingate ushered his sister out.

McConnell heard her say, 'Couldn't Mr Simms be mistaken?'

He didn't catch Wingate's reply but he was pretty sure what it was.

FOURTEEN

'It's goddamn disgusting!' Tony Lane raised his voice above the noise of the crowd in the Bull's Head saloon. He drank half the contents of his glass of beer. 'A goddamned stranger rides into town and then robs a distinguished citizen like Mr Simms. Not only robs him but assaults him too! Mr Simms could have been killed! And what do we do about it? Nothing!'

'He is in jail,' one of the men gathered round Lane said. 'And his trial is due day after next.'

Lane flung some of Vernon's money down on the bar. 'Drinks all round,' he said in an aside to the bartender. A little way off he could see Franklin and Poynton carrying on their own conversations with some of the younger men in the saloon. Both their faces were alight with anticipation. Lane didn't particularly feel the same way. He wasn't thinking of anything much except the jingling of Vernon's money in his pockets.

He turned back to his audience. 'That's as maybe. What do you think he'll get? Five years, ten years? That's not enough. Outlaws get off too lightly these days. Why in the old days we'd have known how to deal with someone like McConnell, without having to resort to the law.'

'But we have got the law now. We can't go round taking it into our own hands. It wouldn't be right.'

Lane sighed inwardly. All very well for Vernon to say it would be easy – buy 'em a few drinks, get 'em likkered up and they'd be ready to lynch McConnell. Things had indeed changed and people in Medicine Creek were, on the whole, law-abiding. It wasn't going to be easy at all. Lane would probably have to spend a lot more of Vernon's money than the man intended. Not that Lane minded that, serve the mean bastard right.

'Well I say we ought to do something and now! Show these thieving outlaws they can't get away with it.'

By standing on his bunk McConnell could just about see out of the cell's tiny barred window. Not that he liked what he saw. For the past hour or so, he'd listened to the growing noise of men shouting and yelling. Now there they were, twenty or so strong, gathered in front of the saloon across the way, their faces lit up in the light spilling out behind them. They looked and sounded ugly.

A noise behind him made him jump but it was only Bart Wingate. 'What's going on?' His apprehension wasn't helped because Wingate wore not only his holstered Colt but another revolver stuck in the belt of his trousers. He was carrying a rifle as well.

'Tony Lane is over at the saloon. He's spouting a lot of nonsense about you.'

Oh God. He wasn't just going to go to jail, he was going to be lynched. McConnell jumped down from his bunk and came over to the bars. 'Can't you stop him?'

'I hoped it wouldn't go this far,' Wingate admitted. 'I didn't think anyone would listen to him. But he's been buying drinks all evening and several of the town's rowdier elements are now in agreement with his demands to see you taken out and hung.'

'You won't let them do it, will you?'

'Not if I can help it.'

'At least give me a gun, let me defend myself.'

'No.'

Wingate's deputy poked his head round the door. 'They're coming, Bart.'

'Please,' McConnell moaned.

'You just stay put and stay quiet.'

'I can't exactly go anywhere can I?' McConnell said but Wingate had already disappeared back into his office. Andrew stood at the bars, rigid with fright. Two men couldn't stand up against a mob, perhaps they wouldn't want to, wouldn't be prepared to shoot their neighbours just to protect a stranger. Vernon was about to get him killed.

Flanked by his deputy, Wingate stepped out onto the sidewalk as the men marched across the street from the saloon. Tony Lane was in front, with Dennis Franklin and Mal Poynton beside him. Wingate wasn't pleased to see Franklin. He had a wild look about him, seeming quite likely to take it into his head to start shooting from the anonymous safety of the crowd. He was the one to watch out for. The rest were townsmen, with a sprinkling of the odd cowboy or two, only willing to cause trouble because they'd had too much to drink.

'Stop right there!' Wingate yelled and raised his rifle, so that everyone could see it.

The crowd faltered to a pushing, shoving halt in the roadway.

Amid several yells of agreement, Lane shouted, 'Give him to us Marshal. We want the bastard to get what he deserves.'

'There'll be no lynching in this town. Mr McConnell will get a fair trial and serve whatever sentence the judge gives him. And that's the only sentence I'll enforce.'

'It ain't good enough. Hand him over.'

'Yeah come on Marshal,' that was Franklin, almost bouncing up and down with excitement. 'Let us deal with him.'

'Don't listen to these men. You're all decent friends of mine. I don't want to shoot you.'

'You won't shoot your neighbours for that sonofabitch thief in there,' Lane sneered.

'I will if I have to.'

'No you won't.' Franklin again. 'You ain't got the guts.'

'Well you'll be the first to find out about that Franklin because you'll be the first one I aim for.' Wingate glanced over at his deputy. The man looked white and scared but Wingate was thankful to see that he appeared determined to stand by his boss. Which was lucky. Bart wasn't sure whether together they'd be able to stop the mob breaking into the jail; he was damn sure he couldn't do so on his own.

'Don't listen to him! He won't stop us!'

The crowd surged forward and Wingate let off one round of the rifle, the slug kicking up a spout of dust in front of the men. Some of them came to a startled halt, almost pushed over by those behind. Eventually order was restored. When it was,

Wingate saw that Franklin no longer appeared so cockily confident but had half-hidden himself behind his foreman.

'I want you all to go on home. Let's forget about this. Otherwise you'll find yourselves in the cells tomorrow morning. Think about the disgrace of what you're doing. The shame you'll feel. The shame you'll bring on your families if you lynch a man, especially one who hasn't even killed anyone himself.'

'He attacked Mr Simms,' Lane yelled but he could tell from the shuffling going on around him that he was rapidly losing ground. The men had been at fever-pitch over at the saloon. They were now having second thoughts. Indeed several people at the edges of the mob were already slipping away.

Besides, here they were facing a Marshal Wingate they didn't know. On the whole, Bart was an affable young man, ready to listen to those with troubles. Tonight those confronting him had found out that when faced with law-breakers of whatever kind he was completely different. His face was hard, eyes steely and there were few who doubted he would shoot them to protect his prisoner.

And he was right as well. Lynch-mobs were all very well in certain circumstances. Those circumstances didn't prevail here in the quiet town where there was a good system of law and order.

Slowly, with hangdog expressions, the men drifted away, hurrying when out of sight so as to put distance between themselves and the madness they had almost committed.

'You too Lane,' Wingate ordered, pointing his

gun directly at the foreman. 'I don't know what you thought you were up to but I want you to know that your kind ain't welcome round here. Go back to the Rocking V and sober up. And be careful in the future.'

'You ain't letting 'em get away with this are you?' Franklin screamed in frustration.

'Ain't nothing I can do 'bout it.' Lane knew when to accept defeat. Franklin appeared ready to rush Wingate and the deputy and Lane caught his arm, pulling him away. 'Come on Dennis. It's too late.'

'Aw hell! Old man Vernon ain't gonna like this.'

'Keep your goddamned mouth shut!' Lane warned but it didn't matter. The two lawmen had already gone into the office and shut and locked the door firmly behind them. There was nothing to do but leave.

Wingate sat behind the desk, laying the rifle in front of him, putting his head in his hands for a moment. Christalmighty! He didn't want to have to do that sort of thing too often.

'Here, Bart,' the deputy said, putting a mug of coffee in front of him.

And when Wingate tasted it, he was pleased to find that the other man had put a liberal shot of something considerably stronger than coffee in it.

In his cell, McConnell could also have done with some whisky, but no one thought of him.

Shivering he sat down on his bunk, legs having turned to jelly. He wiped his forehead free of sweat. That had been a near thing. And by it Vernon had shown his hand. Scared McConnell would tell everyone what Roy had once been and done, and no longer content with just sending him back to jail, Vernon had again decided he wanted him dead. And knowing the bastard he wouldn't give up after one failed attempt. Unless he could do something about it, McConnell was a marked man.

The following morning Julie got up as quietly as she could, careful not to disturb Roy, who, lying on his back, snored loudly beside her. A few hours ago when he got back to the hotel, he'd been in a snarling bad temper, ready to use physical violence; with the hangover he'd undoubtedly have when he woke up, he'd be in no better a mood.

Last night from the hotel, she had watched the mob form in front of the saloon. It had been a long time since there had been a lynching in Medicine Creek but she remembered vividly its horror and the dreadful aftermath. When the men marched over to the jailhouse, she was scared Bart would be hurt. But her brother handled them bravely and eventually they'd dispersed. It was that, she was sure, was the reason for Vernon's mood. Lane had been in the forefront of the mob and after what she'd learned from Andrew McConnell she had no doubt that he was there on her husband's orders.

She left the hotel and began to walk up and down, staring in store windows. Not that she was looking at the goods on display. She was worried about Andy.

She wondered why she should believe him over her own husband. He could be lying about everything but she knew he wasn't. She liked and trusted him. Although he was a bank-robber who'd served ten years in jail, there was a gentleness about him. He was ... nice. He'd left his home and family and started on the outlaw trail because of

Roy, and Julie knew from bitter experience how easy it was to be fooled by Roy and his smooth lies.

It seemed so unfair that Andy was going to be sent back to prison for something he hadn't done, and all because of Roy. Yet what could she do about it? She was scared of Roy; there, she admitted it. And in admitting it, Julie also found a core of courage deep within herself. Whatever happened, whatever Roy did to her, there were times when it simply wasn't right to sit back and do nothing. She had to help Andy. She would help him.

The decision made Julie came to a halt on the sidewalk to find herself outside of Mr Simms' store. Peering through the window she saw that the man was alone. She'd go in and speak to him about what had really happened.

'Here,' Wingate brought in McConnell's breakfast and a cup of coffee. The coffee was Wingate's own evil brew but McConnell had eaten well since being in jail because the food was prepared by the cafe owner.

'Thanks,' McConnell reached out for the tray. His hand caught its edge and it, plate of bacon and beans, coffee, all fell to the floor with a clatter.

Wingate made an instinctive grab for it and at the same time McConnell grabbed him. He pulled the Marshal close to the cell bars and snatched for his gun. Wingate tried to jerk away but McConnell had the gun out and jammed into his side before he could.

'Now, Marshal, just ease the keys from your pocket and pass them through to me.'

'You won't shoot.'

'Won't I? Care to take the chance? Come on, Bart, be sensible.'

Left with little choice, he didn't really believe McConnell would pull the trigger but, no, he didn't care to chance it, Wingate pushed the keys through the bars into Andrew's hands. McConnell shoved him away and, still keeping the gun pointed firmly at him, fumbled with the key and the lock, finally managing to open the door.

'You stupid bastard!' Wingate exclaimed angrily. 'You won't get away with it.'

'Better a chance like this than the certainty of the trial or getting lynched. Someone is out to get me and just because he failed last night, don't mean he won't try again.' Perhaps he was making a mistake, running like this, but McConnell couldn't stay in jail waiting to be murdered. Nor could he face Judge Neely.

'Someone? Who? Lane?'

'No. Never mind. Anyway I doubt you'd believe me about that any more'n you do about anything else. Now come on, stop wasting time. Step over here and get in the cell. Carefully.'

McConnell moved out of the way as, scowling, Wingate went by him and into the cell. McConnell clanged the door shut and locked it, removing the key, throwing it on the floor out of the Marshal's reach.

'You fool!' Wingate's cry followed him as he went through the door into the office.

Nobody was there. Hands shaking, heart beating wildly, he quickly opened drawers in the Marshal's desk, until he found his gun. He buckled it on, scooped up some ammunition as well as a few other bits and pieces that might come in handy. He guessed his money resided in the safe in the corner. No way could he get that.

Wingate's hat lay on his desk. Andrew jammed it on his own head, pulling it low down over his eyes. It wasn't much of a disguise but it would have to do.

He'd delayed long enough. If anyone was to come through the door now, they'd be entitled to shoot him down.

Peering out of the window, he saw a few people across the way, several cowboys riding up and down the street, a wagon making a slow progress towards the feed and grain store. A horse, he guessed it was Wingate's, was tethered to the rail outside the jail.

Followed by Wingate's yells, which couldn't be heard once he'd closed the door, McConnell walked quickly to the horse. Patting its nose, he freed the reins, swinging up on its back. Then, throwing aside all caution, he jammed heels into its sides. Squealing, it took off down the street. No sound of pursuit followed him.

'Hallo, Mr Simms.'

'Oh hallo there, Julie, what can I do for you today?' Mr Simms looked up from the counter where he was arranging a display of glass jars.

Julie had known the man for years. He had owned a store in town for as long as she could remember. When she was a little girl, he'd always had a stick of liquorice or a small toy ready to give her. She knew him well. And today she could tell he was ill-at-ease in her presence. He refused to meet her eyes, his hands fidgeted. And although he smiled, it was nervously.

'I was so sorry to hear you were robbed.'

'Yes, it was dreadful. So frightening when that awful man hit me.'

'I suppose it happened in here? It's very dark isn't it? How could you see Mr McConnell so clearly as to identify him?'

'I had a candle with me.'

'You know, Mr Simms, I can remember a few months ago when your store was losing money. You feared you'd go out of business. I believe my husband gave you a large loan didn't he?'

'What are you saying?'

'I hope your conscience will make you tell the truth under oath on the witness stand.'

Mr Simms opened his mouth, closed it again, went red and resorted to blustering. 'I hope you're not accusing me of lying. Your brother believes me.'

'I'm not saying you're lying voluntarily, Mr Simms, merely that for some reason I think you've agreed to lie for my husband.'

'Oh Julie, please.'

The man looked close to tears. Julie felt sure that he didn't like what he was doing but had been forced to do so by Roy threatening to call in his loan, so putting Mr Simms out of business.

She didn't like hurting the old man, but McConnell's freedom was more important. But before she could press him further, shouts and yells came from across the way. She hurried to the door. Bart stood on the sidewalk, bare headed, gesticulating wildly to those who'd gathered round him.

'What's happened?' Julie asked a man standing near to her.

'Seems like the prisoner overpowered your brother, locked him up and escaped!'

'Oh the damn fool!' Julie exclaimed out loud.

FIFTEEN

Andrew McConnell lay on the ridge overlooking the headquarters of the Rocking V. He was well hidden amongst the rocks, keeping his head down.

When he'd fled from jail, while he knew his best hope of escape was to ride as far and as fast as he could, he also knew he couldn't let Vernon get away with all his lies and deceit; the attempt to have him killed. Vernon had shown McConnell no mercy. Why should McConnell do so for him?

The fact that Vernon would be hiding at the ranch, worried and scared, was no longer enough. McConnell wasn't a particularly patient man, and what little patience he possessed had about run out.

But what could he do?

Did he really want to kill Vernon and be wanted for murder? Wanted for robbery and escape from prison was bad enough. He thought of Julie as well. She'd expressed her belief in him; a belief she would no longer hold if he gunned down her husband.

It was two days since McConnell's escape. He'd ridden towards the foothills between Medicine Creek and the Rocking V, not stopping until he realized that the horse couldn't go on much longer.

121

He'd come to a halt by a stream, letting the animal
drink, doing so himself, filling up the canteen tied
to the saddle pommel with the clear, fresh water.

He'd seen no sign of a posse, but men, led by
Marshal Wingate, had to be out after him. He'd
done his best to hide his tracks – riding along the
bed of the stream, keeping to the rocky ground.
Despite his precautions he felt certain that if
Wingate was experienced at tracking he wouldn't
find it difficult to follow him.

The first night out he'd come across an empty
farmhouse. Empty of people that was, not of
furniture or food. Perhaps the farmer and his wife
were in town for the trial. He'd broken in, cooking
himself up some bacon and beans, and slept in the
farmer's bed. Around dawn, he left, taking with
him some tins of food to see him through.

But they wouldn't last long. He had a Colt 45
and a pocket full of bullets, but no rifle with which
to shoot anything to eat. He had no money.

Once he'd revenged himself on Vernon he had
to go away as far as possible. Perhaps even down to
Arizona or New Mexico. To do that he had to have
money, food and clothes. In order to get all those
things he could see no alternative but to commit
robbery. What difference did it make anyway? He
was already a wanted man and this time his name
and face would be on a poster.

And then the idea came to him. Why not rob Roy
Vernon? The man must have money around the
house, even if it wasn't as much as he'd promised to
give McConnell. And as Roy obviously loved
money, robbing him would provide a certain sweet
vengeance.

In a roundabout way, McConnell rode to the

Rocking V. Now he was there, he knew he couldn't get any closer without being seen.

There was considerable activity below him, more men than normal remaining round the buildings. Not only Lane, Franklin and Poynton, but the rest, the ordinary cowhands, would also be on the look out for the escaped prisoner who, for some reason, and Vernon would be sure to think up something good and plausible, was out to get their boss. He'd be shot before he could get close.

So, the difficulty was how to get Vernon and his men away from the house so that he could rob it without getting caught.

For a while, he thought about it. He didn't know much about ranching but he knew that there would be several line shacks dotted round the Rocking V's outlying areas, where men stayed to look after the cattle without having to return to the main headquarters every night.

Among the things he'd picked up from Wingate's desk were some matches. If he could set fire to the shacks someone would be sure to see the smoke and Vernon would have to send men to investigate. The more fires he started, the more men would ride out. Not just to put the fires out but to catch the man who had set them. Eventually it was likely Vernon, not wanting to stay at the ranch almost alone, would ride out with them.

It was worth trying anyway.

'Boss! Boss!'

Vernon paused in his pacing up and down. Lane was approaching at a fast run. Now what?

He should have let Lane kill McConnell when he was here, like he and the other two had wanted. If

Lane had followed McConnell and shot him, his
body could have been hidden somewhere off the
trail and never found. All Vernon's troubles would
be over then. Instead he'd devised a fancy scheme
to get McConnell thrown back in jail. And it had all
gone wrong. Christ, Lane had even bungled what
should have been a simple attempt to get the
sonofabitch lynched.

Whoever would have thought that Wingate
could handle a mob? Vernon had believed that the
Marshal would meekly hand over his prisoner, or
simply run away. Instead he'd done what he was
paid for and protected his prisoner. And then
Wingate, in his turn, had bungled and allowed
McConnell to escape.

When he was Mayor, Vernon decided he'd make
sure that Wingate would never get re-elected. That
was if he ever made Mayor. In the same
circumstances, Vernon wouldn't hesitate to go
after McConnell. He was petrified that McConnell
would now come after him for sure.

'What the hell is it?'

'Boss, there are two line shacks on fire!'

'What?'

'It's true. The two on the East range. Couple of
the men spotted smoke and went to look. They
were too late to save anything.'

'It's him isn't it?' Red faced, Vernon clenched his
fists in fury. 'The bastard! He's responsible for
this!'

'Looks that way, sir,' Lane smugly agreed.
Vernon wouldn't listen to him. He wouldn't listen
to anyone. Now he'd come unstuck and now he'd
be only too willing to ask his foreman for help.

'Christ! What was that stupid Marshal doing to

let him escape? McConnell never had any brains. It should have been a simple job to keep him in jail. Instead of which he's now out there running wild! And everyone will be asking questions as to why he's picking on me!'

'What do you want me to do?'

'Do! Do! Don't ask me such goddamn stupid questions! I want you to take some men and go out and find the sonofabitch! He must be near those shacks. He can't have gone far. Go on, man, and hurry it up!'

'What about you?'

'Leave some men with me in case he turns up here.'

Again Lane hid a smile. For all his blustering, Vernon was scared. And it showed. All his money and power would do him no good, not if he had to face a man with a gun who was out to get him. 'I'll see to it. You can rely on me.'

'I hope so.' Vernon watched the man walk away. Unfortunately the foreman had asked a lot of questions and, in his fright, Vernon had told him too much. Lane had loyalty only to himself, and when this was over and McConnell was dead, would doubtless ask for a considerable raise. Whether he got it or not was another matter. This experience had taught Vernon one thing; he wasn't going to take any further chances with anyone who was a threat.

Lane feared much the same. He'd worked for Vernon long enough to know how devious he was, how willing to do anything to further his ambitions.

But then Lane had his own ambitions and plans.

McConnell urged the horse into a gallop, leaving behind the second burning shack as quickly as he could. He didn't want to be around when Vernon's men came in pursuit. He wanted to be setting fire to the next shack. Keep Vernon worried. On his toes.

He only slowed down when the building came into view. So far he'd been lucky. The other two were empty. He didn't want to risk getting shot by someone who might be inside, neither did he want to hurt any of Vernon's ordinary hands; he had no quarrel with them.

The line shack was like the rest: a small, square building with door and window at the front and no other opening, and a corral nearby. The corral was empty. Easing round the shack's side, he peered through the glassless window at the one room inside. No one.

He went into the cool, dim interior and piled the few pieces of spindly furniture in the middle, putting the bedclothes on top. Then pulling the matches from his pocket, he lit one and dropped it on the pile. The dry bedding caught at once with a satisfactory whoosh and by the time McConnell reached his horse, there were flames coming from door and window.

When Vernon's men reached the other line shacks they should see the spiral of smoke from this burning building rising high in the air.

McConnell grinned.

Time to go back to the Rocking V.

SIXTEEN

Hiding in a stand of brush, McConnell waited as a group of five or six riders galloped by. They were on their way to the third line shack.

This time when McConnell climbed the ridge above the Rocking V, where he'd previously hidden, he saw that hardly anything was going on down below.

A man was going into the barn and smoke came from the cookshack. That was all. It seemed his plan had worked.

Of course Roy Vernon might still be there, hiding in the house. It didn't matter. McConnell would have surprise on his side and this time he'd take no notice of Roy's lies, no matter what he said.

He rode up to the rear of the house, leaving his horse in a stand of cottonwoods where it couldn't be seen from below.

From his previous visit here, he knew the layout of the downstairs' rooms. He also knew Vernon employed a couple of servants. Quietly he let himself in the rear door, finding himself in a small lobby. On one side was the kitchen, while facing him was the hall running the length of the building.

He paused, listening. The place was still, with the

quiet feeling that came with emptiness. Even so, he
drew his gun and, keeping close to the wall, slid
along the hall, looking in the rooms.

First off was a parlour, then the dining room
with the long, gleamingly polished table. Beyond
that he came to a study, with an enormous oak
desk, leather chairs, a bookcase and the smell of
tobacco and whisky.

He tried the desk drawers. They were locked. In
the corner was a safe. Vernon's money had to be in
one or the other. McConnell had no experience of
picking locks or safe-breaking and would probably
have to shoot them open. Before he did so, he'd
better make sure that the house was empty.

Gun held ready to fire, he crept up the stairs. At
the top was a similar front to back corridor lined
with several closed doors. Tiptoeing along the thick
carpet, he put an ear to each. No sound came from
inside. Except the one at the front. It was a
groaning sound, almost inhuman, making the hairs
stand up at the back of his neck.

Andrew reached out for the handle, slowly
turning it, pushing open the door a crack.

'Oh my God!'

Julie Vernon lay on her side on the bed. Her
dress was torn at sleeve and neck, and arms, throat
and face were covered with livid bruises. Eyes
closed, she moaned in pain.

'Julie!' McConnell holstered his gun and went to
the bed, sitting on its edge, putting out a hand to
gently touch her shoulder.

'Go away,' the girl moaned. 'Please.'

'Julie, it's me, Andrew McConnell.'

She looked up at him through puffy eyes, from
which tears slowly slid as she recognised him. 'Andy.'

'Hush, it's all right, honey.' As she began to cry, not just at the pain but at the kindness – the endearment – she had gone so long without, he gathered her into his arms, holding her gently, scared he might hurt her. A great surge of anger flooded through him. He'd seen a lot of things in the past ten years, known a lot of hard men, but none who would do something like this. 'Who did it?' he asked, knowing the answer.

'Roy,' she mumbled against his chest.

'The sonofabitch.' McConnell wished the man was there in front of him. This time he'd have no hesitation in shooting the bastard down. 'But why?'

Slowly Julie pulled away from his comforting arms and stared at him. 'Because of you.'

'Me?'

'He found out I was asking Mr Simms questions about the supposed robbery. He asked me why. And I told him outright I didn't believe you were guilty but that he'd forced poor Mr Simms to lie.'

'Oh Julie.'

'He accused us of being lovers. Then he started to hit me.'

'This is all my fault. If I hadn't come here you wouldn't have been hurt.'

'You're not to blame. It's happened before.'

'You mean he's done this sort of thing before?'

'A couple of times,' Julie admitted mournfully. Never this bad. This time he wanted someone to take his fury and fright out on. I was handy.'

'Christ! Have you told anyone else about the way he treats you?'

'No.'

'Why not?'

'Because if I told Bart, Bart would kill him.'

'Good riddance.'

'There's the shame as well. People would say it's my fault. That I didn't know how to be a proper wife.'

'That's the sort of crap Roy's told you. It simply ain't true. Anyway, what the hell does what others think matter? Nothing's worth putting up with being treated like this. Where is the bastard anyway?'

'He rode out with some of the others. He was in a dreadful state over you.'

'What about the servants?'

'They left when they heard what he was doing to me.'

'Pity one of 'em didn't take a knife to him.'

'They were scared of him as well. He was quite likely to hit them or worse. Oh, Andy, you must go now. He could be back any moment.'

'I ain't leaving you here.' All thoughts of robbing Vernon fled McConnell's mind. Julie came first. 'Come with me, honey. I'll take you to your brother.'

'But Bart'll be after you for escaping jail. You could get shot.'

'No, I won't,' McConnell said more firmly than he felt.

Tears came into the girl's eyes. 'I don't know what to do.'

'You can't stay here.'

'Roy is my husband.'

'For Chrissakes, Julie, see sense! He could have killed you. Surely you don't want to remain married to him?'

'No, I can't stand him.'

'So what's the problem? Anyway I ain't going to let you stay here all alone. You're coming with me.'

The decision made for her, Julie suddenly felt light hearted. She should have left Roy long before this. Now, provided they got away, she'd never go back to him, no matter what he said or did.

Putting his arms round her, McConnell helped her off the bed. 'Are you going to be able to ride?' he asked anxiously as she leant against him, face screwed up in pain.

'I'll manage.'

'Have you got a jacket or something you can wear?'

'There's a cloak in the cupboard. What about my dress? I can't go out like this with it all torn.'

'You'll have to, honey. There ain't time for you to change. Here wrap the cloak round you. It'll be all right. You don't want anything else do you?'

'No. It can all be left behind.'

'Come on then. Just take it slow. I'm here to help you.'

Supporting her, McConnell led the girl out of the room and down the stairs. She made no fuss, but he'd been beaten up enough times to know how she must be hurting.

The bastard! All McConnell wanted to do right there and then was put his hands round Vernon's neck and squeeze the life out of him. Watch him beg for mercy and not get any.

But first he had to get Julie to the safety of her brother. Hoping that Vernon and his men were still busy with the fires and searching for him, McConnell opened the door onto the porch. 'Not far now, honey,' he began when Tony Lane stepped out in front of them.

As Julie cried out, Lane threw a hard, roundhouse punch that smashed McConnell squarely on the jaw. Andrew went flying backwards, crashing into the porchrail. It broke and he fell with a thump to the ground. And lay unmoving. Julie screamed again.

'Shut up,' Lane snarled. 'Well, well Vernon sure saw to you didn't he?' He ran a light finger down Julie's bruised and swollen cheek.

'Please don't hurt Andy.'

'It ain't exactly Andy I was expecting to see up here,' Lane said sarcastically. 'It's you I came to deal with.' He caught hold of her arm jerking her close. 'I've wanted you ever since I arrived on the ranch. You must know that. Perhaps you feel the same way about me?'

Julie tried to pull away. He'd have been too strong for her ordinarily, now as she struggled, her whole body protested in agony and she had to give in. 'My husband will kill you for this.'

Lane laughed unpleasantly. 'Oh, I don't intend to be around when your husband gets back. And nor will you be. You're coming away with me.' And he picked Julie up, slinging her over his shoulder.

'Andy!'

'Be quiet. He can't hear you anyway. And as I'm taking you away from that bastard you married, you ought to be grateful.'

Julie glanced down the slope towards the work buildings. No one else was around. Roy would never have left the place unguarded but somehow Lane, in charge of the men, had managed it so that he was left here alone with her. She was very frightened. She'd never liked Lane and knew that whatever feelings he might have for her, they had nothing to do with love, only lust. God only knew where he was taking her, what he would do to her.

Slowly McConnell opened his eyes. He put a hand to his jaw. Was it broken? He was lying on his back on the ground and for a moment he couldn't think how or why he'd got there. Then he remembered. Lane! Julie! He sat up. Carrying Julie, Lane had almost reached the corral where two horses stood waiting, already saddled and bridled.

Frantically McConnell scrambled up, wincing as a pain swept through his left leg. Ignoring it, he started to run down the slope after them.

Hearing him, Lane stopped and turned.

'Let her go!'

Growling with fury, Lane dropped Julie, clawing for his gun.

Swearing, McConnell skidded to a halt. Left with no choice, his hand dropped to his Colt but even before he had it clear of the holster, Lane's was out, pointing at him and being fired. Julie's scream sounded at the same time as the shot.

McConnell threw himself down, the bullet whining harmlessly over his head. As Lane fired again, he rolled over on his stomach, brought his arm up and triggered off four or five shots. One caught Lane squarely in the chest. With a startled look in his eyes, the man staggered backwards, tried to raise his gun arm again, failed and fell over. He twitched once or twice and then was still.

Breathing heavily, Andrew got to his feet and headed over to Julie. He glanced down at the foreman. He was dead and McConnell forgot all about him.

'Julie, darling, are you all right?' He helped the girl up and she clung to him.

'He was going to make me go away with him.'

'OK, honey, it's over, he's dead. He can't hurt you any more. Let's go. We've got to get out of here. We can use the horses Lane had ready.' Anything to save time. Anxious about Julie and her ability to ride all the way into Medicine Creek, McConnell helped her onto the mare. 'Cling to the pommell, I'll hold the reins and guide the horse.'

Weakly Julie smiled at him. 'It's not far.'

No, he thought, only five hours' ride, and Vernon and his men could be coming after them at any moment.

SEVENTEEN

Roy Vernon stood over the dead body of his foreman. While Franklin and Poynton both looked angry, and the other men with him looked bewildered, Vernon wasn't upset that Lane was dead. Lane had been getting much too big for his boots and it solved his problem that someone else had shot the man when he'd been thinking of doing the same thing himself.

What he was upset – no absolutely goddamned furious – about was the fact that McConnell must have had the nerve to actually come to the ranch; no one else could have done it. And Julie had disappeared. In his jealous rage, Vernon was convinced that he'd been right all along and the pair of them were lovers. McConnell must have started the fires in order to sneak back here and take her away with him.

What Lane had been doing here all alone didn't concern the ranchowner. All he was concerned about was catching up with the pair of them, killing McConnell and getting Julie back, before anyone could see how she'd forced him to hit her.

And, by God, he was going to make sure they both suffered. McConnell was going to die slowly and the way he'd had to chastise his wife the last time was nothing to what he'd do to her now!

But his ordinary cowhands would never approve, they might even try to stop him. Poynton and, especially, Franklin, were different. They'd want revenge for the death of Tony Lane and Franklin, anyway, would be anxious to do a little killing of his own.

'You men, split up and go back and find the others. Tell them what's happened and bring them back here. No, not you two,' he said as Franklin and Poynton went to leave with the rest. When the men were out of earshot, he added, 'You two are coming with me.'

McConnell glanced anxiously across at Julie. She was slumped forward over the saddle, bruises standing out black and purple against her chalk white face, hanging on through determination only. He was worried, scared that, although he had kept the horses to a fast walk, riding might be hurting something inside her.

Yet he didn't dare stop, not for long anyway, because they hadn't come very far, not far enough at all.

Even though it meant a slightly longer route into town, he was heading for the comparative safety of the foothills, where hopefully it would be possible to hide amongst the trees and rocks, rather than be exposed in the open valleys. He kept looking back over his shoulder, sure that at any moment there would be pursuit on the horizon. But when he judged they were almost halfway to Medicine Creek, he took pity on the girl and came to a halt. Dismounting, he helped her from the horse and raised the canteen of water hanging from Lane's saddle to her mouth.

'Sip it slowly. How do you feel?'

'Awful,' she admitted honestly. 'But I'll make it.'

'You're very brave.'

'I'm not. I feel really scared. Roy will kill us both if he catches us.'

'I know. We'd better get on. Can you ride again?'

Julie groaned but nodded and made no protest as McConnell lifted her back into the saddle. As he did so, he caught a glimpse of dust rising into the air from beyond the ridge.

'Oh no.'

'What is it?'

'I think they're coming!' Quickly McConnell urged the horses into the shelter of some cottonwood trees. 'Stay here,' he ordered and rode back to the top of the hill. There, beginning to cross the wide meadow he and Julie had just left, were three riders. 'Dammit!' Quickly he checked the rifle in Lane's scabbard. Thank Christ it was fully loaded. There was no spare ammunition for it, although he had several extra bullets for his Colt.

When he galloped back to Julie, she stared at him with haunted, frightened eyes. 'It is Roy, isn't it?'

'Yeah. Look, Julie, I think you should go on by yourself while I stay here and try to hold them off.'

'No! You'll be killed.'

'If we go together they'll catch us before we reach town. This way we might stand a chance.'

'I don't see how,' Julie said mutinously. 'I want to stay with you. You were the one wanted me to leave with you.'

'That was different. That was when I thought we

could reach Medicine Creek. This ain't a matter for argument.'

'That's right it isn't. I'm staying. Andy, listen, Roy will be anxious to get me back, not only because he's mad and jealous and he'll want to punish me for trying to escape from him but he won't want me to get to town and for Bart to see me looking like this. He'll know what Bart would do to him. So even if he goes after you he'll send someone after me. I'd be caught and taken back to the ranch. At least with you I have a chance.'

'Hell!' McConnell swore. She was right.

'Besides I can help you. I can shoot, and believe me I will shoot! Please, Andy!'

'OK. We'd better go. You'll have to ride at a lope.'

'I know, don't worry about me.' She leant over to catch his arm and pull him towards her. She kissed him lightly and then clung to him, burying her face in his shoulder. 'I love you.'

Marshal Wingate sat in his office. He didn't feel very happy. It had been bad enough being fooled by someone like Andrew McConnell, who, having protested his innocence so vehemently, had then proved his guilt by escaping. Wingate hadn't appreciated being locked up in his own cell. It looked bad, it was embarrassing. Things were then made worse by not being able to find him. Wingate wasn't a bad tracker but not that good either and somehow McConnell had managed to elude him. The posse stayed out a couple of days but having no luck, Wingate had conceded defeat and returned home.

Once there he'd sent off telegraphs to the

lawmen in the surrounding towns giving them McConnell's description and asking them to look out for him. With luck, McConnell would be apprehended sooner or later.

After that Wingate had gone to face Judge Neely, who was sitting in the room the hotel always kept for him. Despite the fact that he was nearing his seventieth birthday, the Judge had lost none of his overpowering personality nor gruff disposition. He was extremely displeased. Not only had no one met him off the stagecoach but then he'd learnt that the prisoner whose trial he'd come all this way to preside over had escaped from custody and was nowhere to be found.

Wingate had had to endure an uncomfortable half-hour or so, listening to a lecture about duty and responsibility. It was like being a small boy again and it was all he could do not to wriggle uncomfortably on his chair.

Finally the Judge took pity on him and, mellowed by drinking an almost full glass of whisky, said, 'Well I suppose it wasn't your fault. These things happen.' He leaned back in the chair, lighting up a cigar. 'Andrew McConnell, you say?'

'Yes sir.'

'Describe him.'

'He's in his early thirties, tall, thin, brown hair ...'

'Ah yes. I thought the name was familiar.'

'You mean you've tried him before?' No wonder McConnell had looked scared when Wingate told him who the judge was.

'Yes. Ten years ago in Colorado. He was up before me on a bank robbery charge.'

'Bank robbery, Christ.'

'Exactly Marshal. You know I never thought he

was the type. He was scared, looked a lot younger than he was, and should have been back home on his father's farm, not running around, pulling guns on people. I was almost sorry to sentence him. But he'd done wrong and I had no choice.'

'There was no mistake?'

'Oh no. The Sheriff had tracked him from the town to where he was caught. Anyway McConnell admitted it. But,' Judge Neely frowned, 'there were two robbers. The second man was never caught and he got away with all the money. It seems that this man had double-crossed his partner, and left him for the Sheriff.

'McConnell was so naive that for quite a while he refused to believe any such thing had happened. He stated a third person must have come along, knocked him out and forced his partner to leave.' Neely laughed. 'Then at his trial when he realized no knight in shining armour was going to ride to the rescue, he admitted the truth to himself and swore, no screamed, vengeance on this man. Now what was his name ... wait a minute ... it'll come. Vaughan, yes Ray Vaughan, that's it, that's the man McConnell said had left him to take all the blame.'

Now, back in his office, Wingate sighed. It was understandable McConnell wanted revenge on Ray Vaughan, his one-time partner. But had that been what brought McConnell here to Medicine Creek? He certainly hadn't been looking for homestead land. Yet he had been out riding the range, a map in his room marked with the ranches he'd visited. And he'd been out to the Rocking V.

Ray Vaughan, Ray Vaughan. The words hit Wingate's mind like tiny hammers. Was Vaughan anywhere around here? He knew the answer. He'd known it since the Judge had remembered the name. He just hadn't wanted to admit it.

Ray Vaughan – Roy Vernon. It had to be, the coincidence was too great. All that had happened during the past few weeks was too great a coincidence too.

Vernon's previous story about where he came from and how he got his money had been based on a lie. He was a bank-robber.

Except as a lawman, Wingate didn't particularly care about Vernon, but Julie was out at the ranch. If McConnell took it into his head to go out there and seek his vengeance – and God knew he had reason enough to – Julie might be hurt.

Wingate would have to go out to the Rocking V, warn Vernon, put him on his guard, and then look in the vicinity of the ranch for McConnell. Once he had him in jail again, that would be the time to make inquiries about Vernon's past.

Vernon, Franklin and Poynton came to a halt at the crest of the hill. Vernon gave a shout of triumph. 'There they are!'

They watched as McConnell and Julie came out of the shelter of the cottonwoods, heading for the hills.

Vernon was ice cold with fury. 'Poynton you've got a rifle and I hear you're a good shot with it. Shoot my wife's horse.' Let her see what sort of man she'd become involved with. McConnell would leave her and ride off, saving his own hide. He'd make sure Julie was grateful to him for pointing out to her what a lucky escape she'd had from such a coward, and how lucky she was to have such a husband as Roy.

Poynton swallowed nervously.

'Go on man.'

Mal pulled the rifle from its scabbard and rode forward a little way from the other two, raising it to his shoulder and aiming. He had little doubt of his ability to hit the running horse even though it was a long way away. Yet ... supposing he hit Mrs Vernon instead? Or supposing, in falling, the horse landed on top of her?

In his twenty-four years, Poynton had had little to do with women. Certainly, apart from his mother and sisters, he didn't know any decent women. But his family had brought him up to respect ladies, to be a gentleman towards them, and while such an attitude didn't always impress the saloon girls, he tried to do his best to remember his upbringing and he put most girls on the same pedestal as he placed his mother.

He couldn't risk firing and hitting Mrs Vernon. But Christ knew what Vernon would do to him if he didn't shoot. Vernon was about the most unstable person he knew. And not for the first time he wondered how he'd got into this mess and how the hell he was going to get out of it.

He fired the rifle but made sure that he put the bullet well wide of the target.

'You goddamned fool! You missed!'

'I'm sorry sir, I aimed too quickly.'

And now it was too late; McConnell and Julie had reached the far end of the valley and disappeared amongst the hills.

'Shit! Never mind, we'll soon catch 'em up.'

'Let's go,' Franklin urged. He too didn't much like the idea of hurting a woman, although he didn't have quite as many scruples about it as his friend. What he did want was to get his hands on McConnell and kill him.

And the three men started down the hill, spurring their horses into a gallop once they reached the bottom. None had any doubt they'd reach McConnell and Julie before long.

EIGHTEEN

McConnell kept the horses to a steady lope, knowing that to go any faster would be to tire the animals quickly. Now they had reached the foothills, he stayed as much as possible on the slopes where the timber stand was the thickest and provided good cover.

The trouble was he didn't know the lay of the land. Eventually he and Julie came out on the edge of a meadow, stretching wide and long, flat and empty in front of them. He stopped.

'What's the matter?'

'If we go ahead Vernon will have a clean shot at us. But we can't go back. And I ain't sure how long our horses can hold out.'

'What are we going to do then?'

'This is where we'll have to make our stand.'

'Oh, Andy, no!'

'There's no choice. Look, honey, there are some rocks just up ahead, we can hide amongst them. It's our only chance.' McConnell didn't think it was much of a chance but he didn't say so to Julie.

On the other side of the rocks they dismounted and McConnell tethered the horses as far back as he could, where he hoped they wouldn't be hit. Then, pushing the canteens of water into Julie's hands, he took the rifle from the scabbard.

Abruptly, three riders galloped into view round the base of the hill. For a moment McConnell thought of not doing anything, of letting them ride by. He quickly realized that they'd soon discover he and Julie weren't ahead of them. Then they could get behind the hiding place and pick them off at their leisure.

So instead he raised himself up and let loose with a shot. At once their pursuers reined in, threw themselves off their horses and scattered amongst the rocks.

'We've got you now!' Vernon yelled in triumph.

'I wouldn't be so sure of that.'

Several shots came from Franklin and Poynton, making McConnell and Julie hug the ground.

'Mind my wife, I don't want her hurt,' Vernon ordered; he had other plans for her.

'Oh shit,' McConnell said after a couple of moments.

'What is it?'

'Franklin is making his way up the hill, trying to outflank us.' McConnel shot in the man's direction but Franklin dived behind a tree and Andrew didn't think he'd hit him. Immediately he swung back and fired once, keeping Vernon and Poynton pinned down.

But if he was keeping them pinned down, they were doing the same to him and Julie, firing every time they saw a movement, not bothering whether or not they wasted ammunition; whereas McConnell didn't dare waste a round.

When Franklin reached a high point on the hill, he began to shoot at them, wild and fast, yelling with excitement. McConnell flung himself half on top of Julie, shielding her, as leaves and dust flew up in the air and scattered across their bodies. When the fusillade was over, Andrew dodged up again and fired twice more.

'You're nearly out of bullets ain't you?' Franklin taunted. 'We can outlast you easy.'

'Go to hell.'

'Look!' Julie pointed back at her husband and Poynton.

For some reason Poynton was attempting to reach the horses. McConnell had a clear shot at him. He pulled the trigger. Poynton yelled in pain, clutched at his side and went down, crawling on hands and knees towards the safety of the rocks.

'Mal! Mal!' Franklin yelled. 'You bastard!' And he triggered off some wildly inaccurate shots at McConnell.

'It's all right, Poynton's only wounded,' Vernon called. 'For God's sake keep your head.'

'Well that's one down and out of it,' McConnell told Julie in some satisfaction. 'If I can keep 'em from getting any closer until it gets dark, maybe we can ride on again then. If we lose 'em in the hills we can hide somewhere and then come morning ride for Medicine Creek.'

'How much longer until dark?'

McConnell looked up at the sky. 'Hour at the most I reckon.'

The light was fading but unfortunately it didn't fade fast enough for him to put his plan into action.

Suddenly a bullet struck the rocks, chips of stone flew off in all directions, and one hit him on the cheek.

With a cry, he put a hand to his face and rolled

instinctively away onto his back. And a bullet from
Franklin's rifle struck him in the thigh. McConnell
screamed and, with the sudden shock, grabbed for
his leg, dropping his hold on the rifle.

'Andy!'

Through numbing pain, McConnell heard
Franklin slithering and sliding down the hill. 'The
rifle!'

Frantically Julie reached for it and fired at
Franklin as he dived towards the rocks. She missed
and he kicked the weapon out of her hands and
shoved her away so hard, she fell to the ground.
McConnell tried to get his Colt from the holster but
a foot landed heavily on his chest and, as he
blinked up, he saw Julie scrambling to her feet,
fear on her face, while Franklin stood triumphan-
tly over him. The barrel of the young man's rifle
dug into his forehead.

'You're dead, asshole!'

'No! No! Don't shoot him!' As McConnell lay
helplessly on his back, Vernon came into view. 'At
least not yet,' the rancher added, grinning.

'Oh boy am I gonna enjoy this.' And Franklin
poked McConnell with the rifle and then hit his
wounded thigh, laughing as Andrew cried out
again. 'Did Tony scream huh? Did you make him
scream when you shot him? Well I sure as hell am
gonna make you scream before you die!'

For the past half-hour or more, Wingate had heard
the sound of firing. The shots were uneven, frantic
some of them, others single, paced out. They came
from more than one gun; three or four probably,
he thought. And it didn't sound like hunters.

What did it mean?

Although the Rocking V was still a couple of hours' ride away, and the shooting came from the foothills, not from the direction of the ranch headquarters, he bet it had something to do with Andrew McConnell.

Worried, he urged his horse into a gallop. The shooting got louder all the time. And then abruptly stopped. Which made Wingate all the more worried.

'You don't have to do this to him,' Julie begged. 'He'll go away and never come back.'

'Shut up.' And as Frankin dragged McConnell to his feet, Vernon slapped Julie once, hard, causing her nose to bleed. 'Wait till I get you home. I'm going to make sure you never disobey me again.'

Franklin shoved McConnell against the rocks, sticking his gun into his side.

Pulling Julie after him, Vernon stepped in front of Andrew and smiled. 'You've caused me nothing but trouble but now it looks like I've won and you've lost.'

'It's needn't have been this way,' McConnell spoke through clenched teeth, trying not to let the two men know how badly he hurt or how much he was afraid. 'You could have paid me off like you said you was going to. I'd have been willing to leave.' He glanced down at the ground. Through eyes fog-misted with pain, he saw his rifle lying where Franklin had kicked it, too far away to reach, but his revolver was on the ground between him and Julie. Could he get to it? Not with Franklin's rifle digging into him.

'Unfortunately for you, Andrew, I never saw things in quite the same way as you did. Surely even with your limited intelligence you can see I've got too much to lose to let a fool like you lose it for me. If you'd had any sense you'd have played dumb, gone back to jail, been alive. Still I'm quite satisfied. By escaping you played right into my hands.'

'I'll tell Bart the truth,' Julie threatened.

'By the time I'm finished with you my dear, you'll tell your darling brother exactly what I want you to.' And Vernon shook Julie hard. Turning back to McConnell, he went on. 'You're a wanted man, Andrew, and Marshal Wingate will probably thank me for shooting you dead. Save all the money and time a trial would have taken. Of course the townsfolk will have to forego some of their excitement, although seeing your dead body dragged in by me and Franklin will probably make up for that. I daresay even Wingate might ask questions about why I had to shoot you so many times but I'll think of something.' And Vernon shot McConnell in the shoulder.

Julie's scream of 'No!' was echoed by McConnell's own scream as dazed, blinking, he collapsed back against the rocks. He was dreadfully scared.

'Let me! Let me!' Franklin cried. 'Don't make it too quick, please.'

'Stop it, oh stop it,' Julie moaned, trying to pull away so that she could go and comfort McConnell, but Vernon kept a tight grip on her arm. 'Let him go, Roy, I'll do anything you want.'

Vernon laughed nastily. 'That's not much of a promise, because I intend to make sure that happens anyway.'

McConnell didn't know what hurt the most; shoulder or leg. His whole body felt like it was aflame. He found that the worst thing about dying was that Vernon was going to live. His eyes sought Julie's.

With a snarl of jealous fury, Vernon said to Franklin, 'OK then, you wanted to shoot the sonofabitch to death. So go ahead.'

Grinning, Franklin put down his rifle and drew out his revolver. 'Where do you want it then you bastard, huh? In your other leg, for a start.' And he aimed.

Wingate heard the shots and the screams. Now what? And then a couple of horses and a body slumped against the hillside came into view. He jumped off his horse and ran over to it – Mal Poynton! Wounded but still alive. Straightening, at the same time he saw a group of people amongst a nearby pile of rocks – Roy Vernon, the other young man, Franklin, facing, yeah, McConnell, and Julie – oh Christ, Julie – what the hell was she doing here?

Even as he looked across at them, trying to work out what it all meant, he saw Franklin raise his gun. He was going to shoot the already badly injured McConnell.

'Hold it right there!'

'It's Wingate!' Vernon exclaimed in a panicky tone.

Franklin swung round and, in a state of high excitement, didn't stop to think that they could still say they'd captured an escaped prisoner. All he knew was that the Marshal had arrived and would stop him from having his fun. He didn't think of the consequences of his action. All he did was act. He shot several times at Wingate.

'You fool!'

Now what the hell was going on? Wingate dived for the ground and instinctively fired back at Franklin. The young man's body was picked up, seemed to hang in the air for a moment and then was flung to the ground, like a bloody rag.

'Godalmighty!' Vernon swore and stepping backwards let Julie go.

Desperately she dived for the revolver lying on the ground, snatching it up.

'You bitch!' Vernon yelled in frustrated fury. He kicked out at her and as she stumbled, she threw the gun at McConnell.

Somehow McConnell caught the revolver in both hands, and, as Vernon raised his own gun, determined to kill Andrew, he fired first.

Even though he was half-fainting with pain and loss of blood, that close there was no way he could miss.

The bullet hit Vernon squarely between the eyes and without a further sound he collapsed onto his back, landing with a little thump, arms outstretched, mouth slightly open.

'Andy! Andy!' Julie cried, getting up from the ground. She just had time to put her arms round McConnell, before, with a groan, he sank forward onto his knees. He smiled at her weakly and then slipped down, his head nestling in her lap.

'Julie!'

'Bart! Here! I'm all right.'

'What the hell's happened here? My God, Julie, you're hurt! The bastard.' He came to the only conclusion he could – that McConnell was responsible for Julie's bruises; that he had kidnapped her and then shot Vernon, who had ridden to the rescue. He was about to take his anger out on the now-unconscious man lying on the ground, when he came to a halt. Maybe that wasn't right, for Julie had her arms round McConnell and was holding him tight.

'He must be all right, he must.'

Well she couldn't mean Roy, she didn't seem in the least bit interested in him. Puzzled, Wingate pushed his hat to the back of his head, and gave up trying to work it out. 'Julie, what's this all about?'

'It's a long story. I'll tell you once we've got Andy to the doctor's. Please hurry.'

'Fetch the horses.'

Wingate's mind was awhirl with questions. Vernon, shot by an escaped robber who Julie seemed to care about more than her dead husband. Julie, beaten up! Two men dead, another wounded. It was too much to figure out. Someone owed him explanations, and by God he wanted them soon!

NINETEEN

Slowly McConnell opened his eyes. Where was he? For a moment, he wondered who he was – he felt so weak, body hurting all over, so badly he could hardly raise his head. The last thing he could remember was being on a hillside, screaming with pain and now here he was lying in a comfortable bed, a fire burning in the nearby grate, flames shining off log walls. Outside the window, it was light, curtains pulled together to cut out the harsh glare of the sun.

No sooner were his eyes open than there was a bustle of movement and someone came over to hold his hand.

'Julie,' he said, or at least thought he said, for his mouth was terribly dry. He tried to move but couldn't and, groaning, sank back into the pillows.

'Hush, darling.' A smooth, cool hand stroked the hair away from his forehead.

McConnell closed his eyes. Maybe he drifted back to sleep but she was still there, bending over him, holding his hand, when he looked up again.

'Here.' She helped him up a little and raised a glass of water to his lips.

'Where am I?'

'In my home ...'

'The ranch?'

'No, don't worry. My old home in Medicine Creek.'

'I ache everywhere.'

'That's not surprising. You were shot twice. You lost a lot of blood before we could get you back here to the doctor. He'll be pleased to see you're awake. None of us thought you were going to live.' Julie looked like she was going to cry. 'Oh Andy, I was so worried and scared. I thought I was going to lose you.'

McConnell managed a grin. 'I've got a tough old hide. Your bruises have all gone.'

'You've been here two weeks.'

'That long? And Vernon?'

'He's dead. You shot him, do you remember? Franklin is dead too and Poynton is over at the jail, awaiting trial. I feel a bit sorry for him. I'm sure he's not like Franklin and Lane were but just got into bad company. Perhaps the judge will take that into account.'

'And why ain't I over at the jail?'

Julie looked puzzled. 'Oh! The robbery at Mr Simms'. Don't worry. Once he found out Roy was dead, Mr Simms told the truth.'

'What about my escape?'

'Bart has decided to forgive you.' Julie bent over and kissed his cheek. 'Now go back to sleep. I'll stay with you.'

During the next few days, McConnell slowly regained his strength. The doctor came to poke and prod him and express satisfaction with his surgical efforts. Wingate looked in the door and glared at him a couple of times and, as good as her word, Julie stayed by his bedside, helping him, looking after him.

And McConnell came to a decision. 'Julie, honey, I've made up my mind. I'm going home. I know I might not be welcome and if I'm not I'll move on. But I want to see my folks, especially my mother, and see the farm again. I want, if possible, nothing more than to go back to being a farmer. I was a fool ever to leave.'

'Oh, Andy, that's wonderful! I'm certain your family will want you there with them.'

But for all her words, Julie didn't look happy. And as she turned away, McConnell saw tears in her eyes. 'What's wrong?'

'Nothing.'

'Yeah, there is. Tell me. I thought you'd be pleased.'

'I am … it's just that … well you'll be going away and …' Her voice trailed off miserably.

Suddenly McConnell realized why she was upset. 'Hey honey,' he gently reached out a hand to touch her arm, 'don't be silly. I ain't going anywhere if it means leaving you behind.'

Julie turned back to him, eyes shining with both unshed tears and hope. 'Do you mean that?'

'Of course I do. I want you to come with me. Will you?'

'Yes, oh yes!'

McConnell pulled her down on the bed beside him and began to kiss her.

'Stop it, you're not well enough yet.'

'This'll be part of my recovery then.'

'No, it won't, because my brother is going to come home at any minute and he's decided you're strong enough to listen to a long lecture about staying out of trouble. God only knows what sort of lecture you'd get if he saw what you was up to.'

McConnell grinned and held her tightly. 'Who cares?' he said.